THE FLOCKTON FLYER

Look-in Books

THE FLOCKTON FLYER

Peter Whitbread

Illustrated by
Denis Manton

Look-in Books

Jointly published by
INDEPENDENT TELEVISION BOOKS LTD
247 Tottenham Court Road, London W1P 0AU

and

ARROW BOOKS LTD
3 Fitzroy Square, London W1

An imprint of the Hutchinson Publishing Group

London Melbourne Sydney Auckland
Wellington Johannesburg and agencies
throughout the world

First published 1977
© Peter Whitbread 1977

Cover photograph by
Roderick Ebdon

Made and printed in Great Britain
by The Anchor Press Ltd
Tiptree, Essex

ISBN 0 09 915460 9

CONTENTS

CHAPTER 1
AN ODD PLACE TO LIVE

Commander Jack Frost planted his feet firmly apart, cupped his hands round his mouth and roared: 'Ahoy there!' Though he stood only ten paces away from the great iron monster, the sound of clinking and clanking and hissing steam smothered his shouts. He saw a pair of legs kicking between the huge wheels that were nearly as tall as himself and bellowed again, 'Carter ahoy!'

The legs, in stained blue overalls, kicked and wriggled and heaved the body that belonged to them from under the shining dinosaur. Bob Carter stood up beside the Commander in the hot sun and wiped oil on to his face from a filthy hand. They both looked appreciatively at their favourite toy, and she gleamed appreciatively back at them – a fine old 1931, ex-GWR 64 class 0–6–0, pannier tank steam locomotive, with her name in gold letters on her splashers: 'The Flockton Flyer'.

Bob nudged the Commander, 'I've got the whistle working.' Commander Frost's face showed a mixture of delight and disbelief. 'You never!' Bob grinned. 'Like to have a go?' The Commander went 'pssshh' through his lips and stuttered, 'I-I-I'll be cut adrift on an iceberg – wouldn't I just – up on the bridge?' Bob corrected him, smiling, 'The footplate, Commander,' but the old boy hadn't heard him, he was already scrambling up the Flyer's rungs.

Although Commander Frost had been retired from the Navy for ten years, a lifetime afloat had made it difficult for him to adjust. Bob Carter climbed up behind him and pointed to the whistle lanyard. Commander Frost clasped it gingerly and pulled. Nothing happened. 'Harder, Jack – you won't hurt her.' The Commander gave a stronger yank. A glorious melancholy howl filled their ears, rising and falling like a cow elephant in love. Commander Frost looked at Bob, his face full of heavenly joy and awe. 'You hear that, Bob. It's like . . . no, it's more . . . it's finer than any fog-horn you've ever heard.' He gave Bob a look of naughty hope. 'Can I have another go?' Bob nodded – happy in the Commander's happiness.

Far down the line, where Combe Lane bridge humped over the track, Jan and Jimmy Carter paused in their weary climb up the hill from the bus-stop. Beneath them, the line wound down the valley between the Quantock and the Brendon Hills to the north-west corner of Somerset. A distant hoot echoed on the summer air. Jimmy said, 'Dad's playing trains again.' And Jan agreed, 'Keeps him out of mischief. I suppose we'll all be helping again now term's over.' Jimmy heaved his duffel bag, full of the term's bits and pieces, back on his shoulder. 'Pity we couldn't still go to school by train like they used to before the line was closed – save us a two-mile walk.' Jan picked up her case. 'If Dad's taken the day off again, Mum may need help at the garage – come on!' Another lovelorn wail followed them towards the brow of the hill.

Lane End Garage lay on a small rise, along a road that had been busy until the bypass had been built; now the garage looked rather sad and seedy. Behind the pumps and the tiny office was a clapboard shack of a house, whose ageing joints were just about able to cope with all the Carter family.

They all sat round the table in the big kitchen finishing a tasty, if rather obscure, stew which Kathy Carter had made up as she went along. She was an amiable, absent-minded mother, forever brushing long wisps of hair from her eyes and nose and mouth. Beside her, Bob spread his hands on the table. Kathy liked his hands; they made her think of a pair of wooden tools, brown and scratched and stained and oiled and nimble. Jessica, their younger daughter, noticed the hands on the table too, and said in mid-munch, 'Dad's going to make an announcement.' She was always the last to finish, as dainty and precise in her eating as in everything else. Jan and Jimmy caught each other's eye. Jan, active, alert and a bit of a tomboy, was more like her father, whereas Jimmy, the eldest of the three, was slower and more thoughtful. He shared Kathy's deep warm humour, though his was slightly sardonic.

Bob looked round at them. 'Yes. I've two things to tell you – one not so important and one a bit shattering. First – Commander Frost has just told me that the Railway Society had a meeting this morning and decided they can't go on with their plans to open up the line again. They're not short of money, but the track and station need more careful maintenance than most of the members seem to have time for – and we're just not making progress fast enough to please some of them. Anyway, the meeting decided that if things didn't improve in three months they'd have to chuck the whole lot in.'

Bob looked very miserable and his family felt for him. Since the building of the bypass the garage had done less and less business. Bob had spent more and more time working on the engine and rolling stock and track that the Flockton Lane End Railway Preservation Society – otherwise known as FLERPS – had bought from British Rail in an effort to get the line going again. Bob had even taken, and passed, his locomotive driver's certificate – though there had been nothing to drive until he, almost single-handed, had brought the old Flockton Flyer back to life.

Bob's next bit of news, however, really stunned the family. 'Mr Phillips – the owner of this garage – called this afternoon. He's sold it to be pulled down to build a Cash and Carry store for the area. And that includes our house.' The family were quiet. In the pause, a voice screeched from a corner, 'Oh dear oh dear oh dear!' Jessica turned and said, 'Quiet, Clancy!' Clancy the cockatoo rolled from one leg to the other like a drunken pirate and his heavy lids slid up and down. Then he rattled his beak along the bars of his cage. Kathy spoke first. 'Does that mean we have to leave?' Bob looked worried. ''Fraid so. The house went with the job. We have twenty-eight days. In fairness to Mr Phillips he did warn us about this just before Christmas – but I never thought it would actually happen.' Bob's voice trailed off and he looked at Kathy and the children. 'What does everyone think?'

Everyone thought, but no one spoke. Then Kathy said, 'There are two main problems, aren't there? No job – and no home; though the two go together really. We have to get a home where the work is, so the job comes first. In a way it makes us very free. We could go anywhere.' Jan was excited, 'We could emigrate, couldn't we? Australia or Canada – that'd be fun.' Her father looked worried again. 'The only thing is, Jan, although I'm quite a clever mechanic I never actually got any qualifications. I don't think that would help us abroad, it'd take too long to get started on word of mouth alone.'

Jimmy rubbed his nose. 'Scotland?' As the others stared at him he went on, 'North Sea Oil. Perhaps Dad could get a job on the oil rigs.' Kathy was quick to oppose this. 'No. We'd never see him – and he might get drowned all the time.' The family was amused, then Jan said, 'It's not all up to Dad, anyway. We could all do our share. Jimmy and I could both get some kind of work and when Mum's got her Open University degree she can teach.' Jessica broke in, 'And I could work on a farm – I know a lot about animals.'

'No,' Bob said. 'It's kind of you to offer, but it's more important for you to finish your schooling. Anyway – we don't have to decide here and now. I just want you all to think it over. We'll have another talk about it tomorrow.' Clancy gave a piercing whistle and Jan and Jimmy together said, 'Quiet Clancy!' He rolled his eyes to the ceiling.

Jessica got up and went out the back to feed Pest, the goat. Pest had a pen at the back of the garage and was Jessica's responsibility as she had found the little nanny in the first place, eating old exercise books from the school's rubbish bins. She had brought her home the same afternoon and, although Bob had advertised, no one had ever claimed her. Jimmy had said he wasn't surprised, as her appetite for anything that was swallowable was enormous. 'Whoever had her before probably got desperate and put her out to fend for herself.' Pest was always escaping from her pen and had chewed her way through, among other things, several school books, the stuffing of the sofa, a number of eggs – shells and all –· from the hens that Jessica also cared for, two of Kathy's curtains, an entire roll of toilet paper, a scarf of Jimmy's, most of Bob's cleaning rags and Jan's leather belt. She had even had a go at Clancy's tail through the bars of his cage.

Jessica pushed an armful of hay into the pen and as she watched Pest munch she tried to think of a brilliant idea to solve the family's problems. But it wasn't much good. She thought of a caravan –

but knew that the five of them would need a big one that would cost more than they could afford. And besides, what would happen to Pest and Clancy and the chickens? Jessica decided that one of the others would have to find a way out.

Upstairs, Jan and Jimmy made a few suggestions to each other. Jan thought of building a boat and living on the river, but Jimmy reminded her that they weren't on a desert island, where they could just cut down trees as they liked. Then he had suggested trying to find a cave in the Welsh mountains, just across the Channel, but Jan countered that there wouldn't be much work there for a skilled mechanic. So they both agreed to leave it to the others to find a way out.

Jimmy got busy putting the last licks of paint on a scenic relief of the Flockton Lane End Line. It was very detailed, with the hills and streams and roads marked carefully to scale, and blobs of cotton wool and sponge for woods and hedges. All across the middle, from top right to bottom left, the railway line wound over and under bridges, round hills and through cuttings and there was even a little train and carriages made from matchsticks.

Jan decided to go up to Florey Forest and climb a tree. Whenever she was at a bit of a loss she found that climbing helped her to recover a sense of proportion – she liked the feeling of pitting herself against a physical obstacle when her thinking was confused. As she went out through the kitchen she saw Bob and Kathy talking earnestly together. She called that she would be back before dark, and ran off into the gleaming summer evening. When she came back they were still talking.

Her mother and father were perplexed. A few hours before, everything had seemed so sure, so . . . carrying on. Now they were having to make plans for a complete disruption of their lives. They went on talking, over many cups of coffee, but by the time the dark came, the youngsters all in bed, and the house slid gently into a creaking, warm slumber, they had come to no conclusions. Instead they comforted themselves with, 'Tomorrow is another day' and 'Something will turn up'. Not very helpful.

The family slept uneasily through the velvet summer twilight, dreaming dreams and turning circles in their brains, and were little refreshed when they sat down to breakfast the next morning. Jimmy finished first and slipped upstairs looking mysterious and saying he'd be back in a minute. Bob looked hopefully at Jan and Jessica.

'Have either of you thought of anything you'd like us to do?' Jan shook her head. 'Nothing that would be practical.' Jessica agreed. 'Only make-believe.'

Bob said, 'Well, there's no point in worrying. Something will turn up. After all, we've twenty-seven days left.' He paused, and then added, 'First day of the holidays. Would you all like to come down to Flockton Station? I got steam up on the Flyer yesterday.' Before anyone could answer, Jimmy reappeared, easing his big contour board through the door. The relief map was about a yard long and two feet wide. Bob and Kathy watched astonished as Jan and Jessica helped to clear a space for it on the table.

They all looked at it for a moment; then Jimmy said, 'It was supposed to be your birthday present last week, only it wasn't ready. That screwdriver I got you was only a fill-in present.' Jessica said, 'I thought you were being a bit mean . . .' Bob was filled with admiration. 'It's fantastic, Jimmy. It's all to scale, isn't it?' Jimmy was pleased, but quite modest. 'One in twenty thousand – metric, of course.' 'Are those little brown ants supposed to be cows?' Jessica asked. Jimmy smiled. 'Just for the look of the thing; bits of cork really.'

The family were quiet for a bit, all a little choked at seeing the miniature of the stretch of Somerset countryside they knew so well, and would so soon have to leave. Then Bob gave a great yell that sounded a bit like 'Oooaahayieeeh!' Clancy squawked 'Good grief!' and nearly fell off his perch. Bob stared at the relief and then at Jimmy. He said wonderingly, 'Jimmy – I don't know how you do it. . . .' 'In free expression – we get one hour a week with Mr Cross. Of course, I did a bit on my own as well.' Bob interrupted, 'Not the relief, but the solution to all our problems.' Jimmy looked a bit worried. 'I don't know about that.' Then Bob pointed to the small bits of painted wood and cork that marked the town of Flockton and its railway station. 'Ten miles down the line from Lane End – Flockton!'

Still nobody understood. So Bob went on, 'The Society wants to get the line going. Why shouldn't I work on it full time? I'm sure they could pay me a decent wage – and we could keep an eye out for vandals if we lived on the spot.' Kathy echoed, 'On the spot.' But Jan was quicker, 'The railway station!' Bob nodded, bubbling with delight and hope. 'It's quite deserted . . . Tell you what! Let's all get in the van and go down there now and take a

look. I'll give Commander Frost a ring on the way and ask him to meet us there.' Clancy in his cage said, 'Good boy good boy good boy – ' but by the time he'd finished he was squeaking to an empty room. The family were already outside, piling into the van.

Flockton Station was rather like a fusty old lady with no friends who had let herself go and didn't dress up any more. Grass grew between the lines. Paint on the signs was sun-peeled, and they read 'FL KTO ', 'LA ES', 'GE T M N'. ' LATFO 1', and so on.One or two window-panes were broken and old lumber cluttered the doorways of the station buildings, which had a lonely and desolate air. In fact the whole place had the feeling of defeat about it.

The Carters stood in front of the station Waiting Room on the Up Platform. Bob handed some keys to Kathy. 'I'll keep an eye out here for the Commander. You lot go inside and see what you think.' He stalked off in the direction of his beloved Flyer. Kathy let them in to the Waiting Room and Jan and Jimmy and Jessica immediately separated, each imagining the offices turned into a home – each with their own particular interests in mind.

Kathy looked round the Waiting Room. There was an open fireplace for a start, that was good. The two sets of double doors, one to the yard and one to the platform, might make it a bit draughty, but they could shut one set permanently she supposed. She imagined their rather threadbare carpet on the floor and their worn but comforting furniture filling the room. The walls had various, out-of-date travel posters stuck up on them, and over the fireplace was a huge old mirror. Kathy fancied her dusty curtains, washed and pressed, hanging in the rounded gothic windows, and she began to think it could be very cosy.

At that moment, the hatch to the next door Ticket Office shot up and Jimmy's head poked through. 'Here, Mum! This'd make a smashing kitchen. Look – a serving hatch!' He put on a posh accent, 'Right you are, dear – steak and two veg comin' up *now*!' Kathy joined him through the connecting door and looked round the neat little room. Plenty of shelves, and an old ticket rack that would take plates and pans. Jan opened the door of a great old-fashioned wall safe. 'Look, Mum – a fridge! Dad can wire it up, he can fix anything. Remember the time he changed our old gas

stove into a washing machine?' 'Yes, and nearly blew us all up in the process,' laughed Kathy. 'There are even electric plugs to take the cooker and the kettle!' Jimmy exclaimed. Jan pushed her mother through another connecting door to the Parcels Office, saying, 'Can't you see our three beds in here? There's a basin in the corner with running water, and lots of cupboards!'

A loud wail came from a passage along the back. Jan, Jimmy and Kathy looked at each other. 'Jessica!' Then they dashed into the passage. Up the far end stood Jessica in front of three vast ancient lavatories with brass fitments and slot boxes on the outside of the doors. She turned to them in dismay. 'Mum – will we have to spend a penny every time we want to spend a penny?' They laughed and Jimmy said, 'You'll have to start making a collection right away. They take old pennies, you know.'

Jan looked through a grimy window into the station yard where Commander Frost had extricated himself from his sleek Renault and was talking to Bob, who was waving his hands about excitedly. Jan said, 'I think our future's being decided already.' The others sobered up and together they walked back through the Ticket Office and Waiting Room and out into the yard.

Bob and Commander Frost came over to them. The Commander squared up, feet apart, hands in jacket pockets, as if to make an announcement from the bridge of his ship. He cleared his throat like a speedboat starting up and went on to speak in jerks, missing on one cylinder. 'Bob's told me – good idea – good for all of us – can't give definite answer till I've sounded Board – but feel sure they'll agree – my advice – get moved in and batten down hatches – possession nine points of law – never did like chat – Hell's teeth! – believe in action – once yer in they've got to get yer out, ain't they? If I were you I'd drop yer anchor and unload here first thing tomorrow.'

Bob looked at his expectant family. 'Or this afternoon?' They shouted excited agreement, and Bob went on, 'Right – you take them back in the van, Kathy – I'll get steam up on the Flyer and meet you back at Lane End at four o'clock. Right?'

'Right!'

Then, as the four of them turned away towards the van, Commander Frost, looking very pink, brought his voice down to a fortissimo whisper. 'Er . . . Carter – that is Bob – I . . . er . . . would you mind . . . er – no chance of – eh? Hey?' Bob's lips twitched.

16

'You want to be my fireman?' Commander Frost's face filled with a wonder inexpressible – like a deprived child suddenly given a five-pound box of soft-centre chocolates. 'Ooooh – do I just? Lead me to her!'

And so Bob did. Two lads together, Bob Carter paterfamilias and fadger extraordinary, and Commander 'Jack' Frost, Royal Navy retired, Chairman of the Board of the Flockton Lane End Railway Preservation Society, walked purposefully towards the shining beauty that stood proudly in the siding. They stopped and turned as an odd cacophony reached their ears. The van was leaving the yard, and, punctuated by backfires, four jerky voices could be heard singing, somewhat inharmoniously, 'Be it n'ev-er so crumbly . . . there's no-o place like ho-ome . . .'

CHAPTER 2
DEPARTURE AND ARRIVAL

The Carters slumped round the table in the kitchen of Lane End Garage. On getting back from Flockton, Kathy had at once started cooking an enormous potful of stovies. She had used a recipe handed down from her Scottish great-grandmother and added some nourishing variations of her own. Mixed in with the sliced potatoes, onions, and oatmeal were shavings of fat bacon, several hard-boiled eggs and a giant tin of baked beans.

The whole family had returned ravenous from Flockton Station, and even Jessica had had a third helping. Now, full of hot victuals, they found it difficult to comply with Bob's plea for ideas about how to move house from the garage to Flockton Station.

Bob was picking his teeth with a match-stick, which made him speak in jerks. 'It's an annoying distance – twelve miles – too far to shift – furniture bit by bit – and yet – it seems so near to bother with – hiring a big van – which we – can't afford anyway.' Jimmy slurped his tea. Kathy asked him not to for about the six millionth time since he'd been born and Jimmy, not quite hearing as usual, asked, 'How much have we got?'

Bob put his match-stick on his plate and looked at Kathy. She looked after all the cash they had as Bob invariably lost it out of his tool-boxes, and once Pest had eaten two five-pound notes out of his back trousers pocket as he was greasing an axle. Kathy knew exactly. 'We have sixty-nine pounds in the bank and nearly seven pounds in the jam-jar. And your week's wages to come tomorrow.'

Jan forked a last piece of potato off Jessica's plate and, as she chewed, suggested, 'Couldn't we go backwards and forwards in our van?' Bob shook his head. 'It'd need too many journeys – the sofa alone would take one trip – the van's just not big enough.' 'How about a boat?' Jessica suggested. 'It's only a mile to the sea both ends – couldn't we put it all on a barge or something? Across Blue Anchor Bay?' Jimmy stood up so quickly he knocked his chair over. 'Hang on,' he said, and without hesitating to pick up his chair he shot out of the door, letting it bang behind him. The family took little notice; Jimmy often did odd things, in fact they all did, so each other's peculiarities passed without comment.

By the time Bob had finished telling Jessica that it would take a big barge to carry all their bits and pieces, and it might cost as much to hire as a van, Jimmy was thudding on the outside of the door with his foot; Jan opened it and Jimmy side-stepped in, carrying his relief map, and pushed a space clear on the table saying modestly, 'Here, dear Father, is the solution to our difficulties.'

Bob looked suspicious, for Jimmy's solutions had a habit of sticking. 'If you notice,' Jimmy was saying, 'at this end the garage is only half a mile from Lane End Station – and at Flockton – well the buildings are right on it. So . . .' Bob was only a beat ahead of Kathy in seeing the point. 'Load the lot on a trailer behind the Flyer and take it down by rail?' 'Is the Flyer ready to pull a load yet?' put in Jan. 'Oh yes.' Bob was firm. 'She's done very well on the test runs this last week. It's a grand idea!' 'Yes it is,' Jimmy announced with evident satisfaction. 'Just needed a touch of genius, that's all.' In the corner Clancy gave a derisive cackle and Jimmy threatened, 'You'll get left behind – you moulting mothball.'

But Clancy wasn't. The next day they were all up at dawn. Kathy drove Bob down to Flockton in the van, leaving him to get steam up on the Flyer to bring her up to Lane End. Then the Carters pottered to and from the garage and Lane End Station and by eleven o'clock the last load was fastened in, on or around the little van; there was barely room for Bob, Jan and Kathy inside. Jessica, who had volunteered to lead Pest down to the station, watched them groan off, with chair legs sticking out from open windows, buckets with shoes in them, hanging from bumpers, and Clancy's cage – with him inside shrieking awful words he'd picked up from the sailors on Plymouth docks – swinging from the tines of a garden fork that stuck out from the back doors.

The Flockton Flyer stood hissing gently to herself at the down platform, where the station yard gave easy access to the truck trailer that was coupled to the rear of the engine. As the van grunted up alongside, Jimmy, who had remained there roping the load on, clambered down from the high hill of furniture and effects that were secured to the trailer. He opened the door of the van for Bob to slide out, then started to unload by unhooking a dazed Clancy from the fork. Kathy and Jan took the smaller stuff, and quite soon the trailer was piled with every last piece.

There was hardly room in the engine cab for more than three, so Kathy volunteered to ride on top of the load, hoping she wouldn't actually have to hold it together. Bob locked up the van, which their friend Basil Humpthorn was going to drive down later, and heaved himself up into the cab beside Jan and Jimmy. As he did so a plaintive wail came from the top of the load. 'We've forgotten Jessica . . .' And they had. Bob looked at his watch. 'She should have got here by now – it's not that far.' 'There she is,' interrupted Jan, pointing, '*and* with another mouth to feed!'

Sure enough, Jessica had appeared round the corner leading a placid Pest into the yard; in her free hand Jessica clutched a tiny black-marmalade-and-white scrap of kitten, who was mewing incessantly. 'She was lost in the middle of the road and might have got run over,' Jessica panted, 'and she's hungry – I squirted some of Pest's milk in her mouth and she loved it.'

Bob looked down from the cab sighing, 'Another nuisance to bother with; never mind. Pest better come in the cab with us, and, Jess, take the nuisance on the load with Kathy.' Jessica pushed from below and Jimmy and Jan pulled from above, till somehow a reluctant Pest was manoeuvred up into the cab. Jessica scrambled up on top of the load with her mother, the purring kitten clutched tightly against her. 'Oh well,' said Jessica, 'I suppose Nuisance is as good a name as any. . . .' Bob called from the cab, 'All set?' and Kathy yelled confirmation. Then Bob summoned up the power from the Flyer's belly, the wheels turned slowly and the gallant little engine pulled the Carters and all their worldly goods out of Lane End Station, and, gathering speed, puffed importantly down the line on the way to a new and adventurous future.

The length of track that had been acquired by FLERPS ran under the west edge of the Quantock Hills, through the crumpled blanket of summery Somerset farmland, where history was written clearly on village after village of golden stone; cave-dwellers, Saxon markets and Roman villas all helped to tell their story of the ancient kingdom of Dumnonia. The single-line track pottered through field and forest down to the sea at Watchet, busy with small ships and big sailors and lovely views across Blue Anchor Bay to the rainbow cliffs of Flockton.

The family knew the area well. Jan and Jimmy had biked up and down most of the hills and vales between Taunton and Flockton; Jessica, who preferred walking, had covered less ground more thoroughly; Kathy had been making a study of local history for her Open University degree. Bob was the only one who had travelled along the line by train before, so the rest gazed excitedly about them most of the way, pointing out features of interest to one another, until there was a sudden grinding skid as Bob braked hard. The Flyer screeched resentfully to a halt as the family looked down the line ahead and saw an extraordinary figure hunched at the side of the track, near an old platelayer's hut.

It seemed halfway between a man and a scarecrow. As the engine rolled the last few yards, Jan could see a hand, like a twig from a snowman, sticking out of a torn worn sleeve, the thumb indicating a clear wish for transport in the direction of Flockton. Jimmy noticed that layers of coats, waistcoats and pullovers covered the scrawny body, though, as a small concession to the hot sunshine, they were all undone. Among them glinted a gold chain, and the remains of several shirts and vests peeped through a hedge of holes. Prehistoric tweed trousers wrinkled round his legs, their ends tied with binder twine round the tops of short perished wellingtons. On top of his head was a straw hat with a feather in it and lower down were first greasy grey curls and then a hairbrush stubble. Surprisingly, among this accumulation of rags lived a pair of kind eyes and a broad warm, slightly cheeky smile.

21

The man took a halting step or two towards the side of the Flyer. Pest looked down disdainfully and bleated in his face. He stepped back, coughed and spat. 'Any chance of a lift down Exeter way?' Bob blinked. The last thing you expect on a closed country railway line is a hitch-hiker, particularly one of such uncertain age and quality. 'Er – 'fraid not. The line stops at Flockton.' The scarecrow belched deeply. 'Flockton'll do – can I 'op on?' Just at that moment there was a metallic jangle from the underside of the Flyer, followed by a bubbling shriek of steam. 'Ye gods!' cried Bob. 'The pressure's soaring!' The grey crusty face beamed up. 'You dunno wotcher got – do yer? I do. Worked on railways all me life – got an 'ammer 'andy?' Jimmy reached one down to him. 'Sure you can fix it?' Yellow, decaying teeth showed partial encouragement. ''Ave a go, won' I?' A hand like a parched thistle reached up and took the hammer, then the whole apparition vanished under the body of the Flyer.

Jan, Jimmy and Bob exchanged amazed glances, and, on top of the load, Kathy shrugged her shoulders at Jessica's raised eyebrows. 'Whatever it is, it's pongy,' Jessica said. 'I can smell him from up here.' In the cab Jimmy shouted above the hiss of steam, 'What *is* the trouble?' Bob looked glum watching the pressure mounting. 'Blessed if I know – I checked every damn joint yesterday.'

As he spoke, there was a resounding 'Doi-oi-oi-oi-ing!' from beneath them, and at once the steam stopped; in the newly restored quiet the rag-bag popped up again, holding up the hammer. 'All she needed – prod in the guts in the right place.' Jimmy took the hammer back and held out his hand to help the man to his feet. He looked appraisingly round the cab, then back at Bob and said, 'Bill Jelly – wanderer and odd jobber – bin everywhere – done ever'thin' – good little bus you got 'ere.' Bob grinned, 'Welcome aboard – and thanks.' He grasped the regulator and as the engine moved forward again, the heat in the cab began to assume a rich smell that contained strains of wet bonfires, old stew, and stale cheese. The man spat with an explosive hiss into the fire-box. Then Bill Jelly started singing an old, unknown song through his long, thin nose as the Flyer continued on her way towards Flockton.

Commander Jack Frost stood astride four-square in the centre of Flockton Station yard as Bob trundled the Flyer to a halt alongside the station buildings. He roared 'Ahoy!' and a small piece of putty fell from the outside of the Waiting Room window. 'Got news for yer Bob!!' Bob glanced over the controls and jumped down on the platform. 'Better see what he wants. Jimmy, can you start getting the stuff unloaded? Just shove it all down under the platform roof for now, till we work out where it's going.' Jimmy said, 'Aye, aye, sir!' and was dug in the ribs from behind. ''Elp yer unload – many 'ands an' all that – eh?' Bill Jelly winked blearily. Jimmy said, 'O.K. – could you give Mum and Jessica a hand down first?'

Bob strolled back with the Commander towards his car. 'Good news and dodgy news. Saw five out of six of the Board s'afternoon – all in favour you and yours berthin' here – six months' trial.' Bob smiled with relief as Frost went on, 'Fact, yer got more – they want a Grand Opening to the public by next holiday season – say late May early June – so your stayin' here depends on gettin' yer skates on and standin' to.' Bob started to say, 'I don't see why I shouldn't have . . .', but Frost overrode him like a mid-Atlantic wave. 'There's another faggot in the bread basket, though. Gwillim.' 'Oh no! What's Percy up to now?' Bob groaned.

Percy Gwillim was almost the only nastiness in the smooth running of FLERPS. Chairman of the Residents' Association, he had always opposed the reopening of the line – mainly because his house overlooked the station and he had deeply appreciated the peace that had followed the line's closure.

The Commander lowered his voice to an earthquake rumble. 'Yer know he's got that farm down by Combe Florey Halt; now he's on about trains frightenin' his cows off their milkin'.' 'That's rubbish,' Bob replied. 'Cows graze by railways all over the country.' Frost wagged his head, 'Never bin to sea, that's Gwillim's trouble. Oh, we'll get round him all right, but it ain't goin' to be plain sailin'. Few sharp squalls before we get into port. Just thought I'd warn yer – handle him gently if he sticks his nose in.'

At that moment there was a shriek across the yard. Kathy had scrambled down safely with Bill Jelly's help, but Jessica had slipped and slid all the way down the load into his arms, and they'd collapsed on the ground in a tangled heap. Jessica was not pleased, patting the dirt off her dress as she got up. Bill cackled on his back, then looked serious. 'Got to be careful – in my condition.'

Jack Frost was looking across at Bill bug-eyed. 'What in all the seven seas is *that*?'

'We picked him up near Stogumber Halt. I think he wants to help.'

'Funny-lookin' feller – wadger think?'

'Could be useful, moving in at least. We'll see after that.'

'Righto then. I'm off to Stogumber to see Gwillim at his farm – persuade him no damage done. Difficult. Not the most tactful chap.' Bob agreed. 'He's a pain.' But Frost countered, 'Not him – me. I seem to get worked up when people don't see things my way. Not to worry – do me best to sort things out. . . .'

He was halfway into his car, calling out, 'Regards to Kathy and the brood!' and he waved across the yard to them – as if they hadn't heard. They all waved back as he drove off.

By half past three the station buildings were beginning to look like home. Jan and Jimmy were making up three beds in the Parcels Office. Jessica had found an empty coal bunker that would do to keep Pest in overnight, and was counting the hens that she had let loose in a small walled garden area by Platform Two. Nuisance the kitten balanced, hissing, on her shoulder, all her hair standing up. Bob had shunted the Flyer into one of the sheds and damped her down for the time being, and was now putting his and Kathy's bed up in the Station Master's Office. Kathy had got Bob to plug in an electric ring in the Ticket Office and was stirring a huge panful of stew.

She jumped as the Ticket Office hatch slammed up and Bill Jelly's gruesome head poked through. 'Smells very good that – wot is it?' Kathy glugged some brown sauce in as she stirred. 'It's Eskimo broth – I heard it on Radio Two. Of course, I added a thing or two of my own, but basically it's bacon scrapings, fish cakes, whale oil, suet, dried beans and chopped seaweed.' Bill gulped, 'And your lot are goin' to eat it?' Kathy was cheerful, 'Oh yes, they usually do. Of course – I don't tell *them* what's in it.' Bill came round through the door. 'Well . . . I can't go back on meself – it *does* smell good; though I'd like to know where

25

Eskimos get bacon.' Kathy said, 'That was one of my additions.
It's ready now; give them a shout, will you?'

Bob, Kathy, Jimmy, Jan, Jessica and Bill all sat round the table
in the middle of the Waiting Room, sated with Kathy's concoction
and feeling well pleased with themselves. Although there were
lots of small things still to be unpacked, the main move had been
accomplished and already they were beginning to feel at home in
their bizarre surroundings. Bill said unexpectedly, 'Wotcher goin'
to do about baths?' After a moment of stunned silence while they
all wondered at Bill's sudden interest in cleanliness, Bob answered,
'I'm fixing up a shower in one of the old WCs – it'll be quite the
thing when I've finished.'

'What do we do with the rest of today?' asked Jan. Bob con-
sidered, then said, 'I think we've earned a rest. The beds are
ready for tonight and everything else is at least under cover. We
can finish unpacking tomorrow.' He looked across at Bill Jelly.
'There's work here for you tomorrow if you want it. We've
carriages to paint, the station to clear up, track to lay and so on.
We can't pay much, I'm afraid, but at least we can feed you and
you can sleep on the sofa in here.'

Bill shook his head. 'Familiarity breeds content – dunnit? I got
a cosy little roost in that 'ut up the line. I'd enjoy 'elpin you out,
though, and feedin's all I ask – Eskimo's broth an' all!' Jimmy
asked, 'You said you'd worked on railways all your life?' Bill
picked a bit of fish cake off his chin and put it in his mouth. 'Part
of all my life – yes. Bin everywhere – done everythin' – railways –
ships, cattle ranchin' – diamond mines – China, India, South
America; there ent nothin' I ent done nor nowhere I ent bin.'
Jimmy winked at Jessica. 'Useful man to have around.' Bill
agreed: 'Ho yus – I bin in a few tight corners. . . .'

Jan got up and began clearing up. The others started to help
her collect plates as Bill slid out on to the platform. He took a
burned-out pipe from one pocket, a tin of tobacco from another,
and a box of matches from under his hat – always the driest place.
After he had lit up he sprawled on a platform bench, puffing
contentedly. Jan came out from the Waiting Room and stood
near him, irresolute. Bill looked up. 'Loose end?' Jan said, 'No –
the opposite really – there's so much to get used to I don't know

where to begin.' She looked at Bill. 'Are you going back to your hut now?' He nodded through smoke and Jan blurted out, 'Can I come and have a look?'

Bill Jelly coughed, choked, wheezed and spat. Jan thought he was going to collapse till she realized he was laughing. Not seeing what the joke was about, but suspecting it might be her, she was on the point of leaving when Bill cut in. ''Aven't your mum and dad warned you about goin' off with strange men?' Jan smiled. 'You're not strange. Peculiar perhaps, but – anyway, I trust you.' Bill wiped his eyes. 'Righto, Jan, but wot about the others?' Jan shrugged. 'Jimmy wants to get his books in order on the shelves and Jessica's washing and ironing – she often is. I like to be doing things more. I told Dad where I would be.' 'Right you are, then!' Bill moved off down the platform and Jan followed.

They walked up the track together, not talking. It was an enchanting stroll. The heat of midday was giving way to the cool of late afternoon, freshened even more by a breeze off the wide estuary of the Bristol Channel that gleamed blue through the trees on their left. Jan only spoke once – to ask Bill why he wore so many clothes at the same time. His cryptic reply was that it saved 'taken' them on and orf'. It was about three-quarters of an hour before they reached the hut, and Bill opened the door with a bit of a flourish and showed her inside.

It was surprisingly neat. An old iron bedstead filled one corner, sporting a mattress off a dump, covered with a motley collection of old rugs and blankets. Wooden boxes did for tables, and sawn-off tree-trunks served as stools. Coloured travel posters were stuck on the walls. The two tiny windows had sacking curtains and the original iron stove was glowing low, with a large kettle simmering upon it. 'Cup o' tea?' Bill asked, and Jan nodded. She sat down on a box whilst Bill tinkered with mugs and jugs and spoons. He looked at her through rheumy eyes that were warm with kindness. She seemed troubled, and very vulnerable. 'You want to say somethin' – you on'y to open yer mouth.' Jan hesitated, and then all at once found herself talking as she hadn't done for months.

As they sipped tea she told Bill how fed up she was at school, mainly because she couldn't make up her mind what to do when she left. She grumbled about most of the active jobs being taken up by men. Jan told him how much she wanted to travel – but not

27

as a secretary; she wasn't mechanically minded enough to help on the railway as much as she'd like, and she didn't fancy doing refreshments. She explained how keen her father was on trains – 'just like a small boy' – and how her mother was busy with her studies for Open University. Jessica seemed completely taken up with her animals and her appearance. And Jimmy, the one Jan had most in common with, seemed fully occupied with his books and models.

'I'm just so restless, Bill,' she went on. 'If only we had emigrated. But now we're here, stuck with Dad's great dream of shunting engines with paying passengers up and down Somerset forever. And we don't even know if that will succeed. Now he's got his mind fixed on a splendid, great Grand Opening with bands and flags next spring, but there are people against him. Is it all going to be worth the effort?'

Bill let Jan tail off, which she did as she became a little embarrassed by her own chattering. Then he said, 'Adventure's what you want, ennit?' Jan nodded, hopeful, excited. Bill went on: 'I can tell you then that adventure only comes when and where it's looked for. You sit back and wait for things to 'appen – nothin' will! I've 'ad my share of adventures. Too much sometimes. And here its brought me to a mad family livin' in a railway station playin' trains. But it wouldn't 'ave 'appened if I 'adn't stuck me thumb out and asked for a lift. Now would it?' Jan agreed. 'But how do you start?' Bill grinned and did a hitching sign with his thumb. 'That's all very well, but you've got to find something to stick your thumb out at!' Jan argued. Bill laughed. 'You're sharp all right. Though you ent got nothin' to worry about. I don't mind bettin' that so long as you keep your eyes open and yer brain clickin' you'll find enough adventures this next year to keep you 'appy the rest of yer life . . . just thinkin' of them. Now – you get on 'ome.'

Jan got up, feeling better already. Bill added, 'Any time you want to 'ave a chat, come out 'ere – or even if you just want a lonely place to sit and think when it's rainin' and I ent 'ere. Be my guest.' Jan smiled gratefully from the doorway, then turned and ran off, back down the track. Bill Jelly put eight more teaspoons of sugar in a second mug of tea and stirred thoughtfully. 'Adventure . . .' he chuckled wheezily, '. . . it's all round yer – ennit?' And he slurped sweetly, relishing each swallow.

CHAPTER 3
THE SHOW MUST GO ON!

Outside the Waiting Room fog mingled with October dusk to make a mysterious half-world of shifting shadow. It was All Hallows Eve, and inside, bright with fire and lamplight, Jan was busy finishing off a German exercise, the start of her 'A'-level work. Jimmy had completed his homework and was painting wooden signs to put up on the Nature Trail the family had mapped out between the coast and the Quantock Hills. They hoped that prospective passengers on the Flockton Flyer would take time off to follow ancient paths and rediscover tracks that wound through prehistoric burial grounds, past Roman villas and medieval battlefields, and all through sweet Somerset scenery.

Kathy was reading about the Battle of Sedgemoor. She was interested to learn that it was the last battle to take place on English soil, fought in 1685, between the rebel Duke of Monmouth and the forces of the Crown. She thought she might go and see the site one day – Sedgemoor wasn't far away – just the other side of Hardington. She pushed her specs back on her nose and said to Jimmy, 'It's amazing how much happened around here when you really go into it.' Jimmy thought it must be the same anywhere - it was just that people didn't notice.

Jan closed her German grammar with a tired sigh. 'Where's Jessica?' Jimmy grinned. 'Studying her Japanese flower arranging in Parcels. As fast as she sticks her old man's beard in, Nuisance nibbles it out.' Kathy closed her history book. 'It'll be time for supper soon.' Jimmy said, 'Don't tell me! It's frogs' legs and Chinese chips.' Kathy smiled sweetly. 'How did you guess?'

At that moment there was a loud bang outside, like a large paper bag bursting. Jimmy jumped and spattered paint on the sign he had been painting with the words: Osric's Barn. The sign had a pointed finger on it which now looked as though it had chicken-pox. He and Kathy and Jan exchanged resigned glances. Jessica appeared through the door from the Parcels Office looking cross. 'Dad still playing with his detonators?' Jan said, 'Yes – they could be necessary if we often get fog like this. Let trains know they're at a terminus.' Jessica objected. 'But ours is the only train that runs on this track and we *know* it's a terminus.' Jimmy wiped spots from the sign, winking at his mother. 'Try telling Dad that.' Kathy said: 'Come on, Jess – you can help me with the supper.' She looked at Jimmy – 'Bread sandwiches!'

Jessica followed her mother into the Ticket Office and began clattering pans about. Soon there was another bang outside. Jessica said, 'I'd better make sure Trivet's all right – he might hurt himself if he starts panicking in the stable.' Trivet was the most recent of Jessica's acquisitions in the four-footed line. She had found him wandering along the track at Combe Florey one day, and though they had advertised, no one had come forward to claim him, much to Bob Carter's chagrin. As Jessica opened the door to the platform, a figure loomed up out of the foggy dark and pushed past her into the Waiting Room.

'What the hell's going on now?' It was Mr Percy Gwillim, Chairman of the Flockton Residents' Association, treasurer of the Round Table, local dairy farmer and, in his own opinion, quite the most important person for some miles around – if not in England. During the last few months he had done everything he could to stop Commander Frost and the Railway Society from getting on with developing the line. His chief objection was the noise of track laying and of the trains going past his house. Now he glared at Jimmy and Jan and grunted, 'Eh? What? Humph?' He was tall and thin with a beaked nose and tiny eyes and very little hair. A squawk from the corner made him jump as Clancy squeaked, 'Wotcher cock?', and Jan and Jimmy together said, 'Quiet, Clancy!' Then Mr Gwillim jumped again as the hatch slammed up and Kathy poked a floury face through from the Ticket Office. 'Do sit down and make yourself at home, Mr Gwillim – my husband will be in in a moment.'

'Certainly not. Haven't got time – just tell me what these disgraceful explosions are about.' Jimmy said, 'Dad's doing a test run for excavating a tunnel under Hangman's Hill.' Mr Gwillim was speechless – his farm stood on that hillside. Jan thought he was going to suffocate and said quickly, 'You have to get used to Jim's jokes, Mr Gwillim – we all do. It's only Dad trying out detonators for the fog.' Mr Gwillim at length found his voice, thickened with anger. '*Fog?* Who cares about fog?' Kathy poked through the hatch, 'You would, Mr Gwilim, if your animals got lost in it and we had to come up the line and help you out.' She blew flour off her nose and disappeared.

Before Mr Percy Gwillim could find a reply, Bob Carter came through from the platform smiling happily. 'They work,' he called out; then he noticed Mr Gwillim glowering. 'The man's called to service the refrigerator,' Jimmy said, and then ducked through to the Parcels Office. Mr Gwillim choked. 'This is the last ultimate straw – d'you hear? We had five years of peace here before you idiots started clanking up and down again in your great iron monstrosities. Well, I've had enough, d'you hear?' Bob made an effort to keep his temper. 'I hear you, Mr Gwillim, very well. They can probably hear you in Taunton. Now why don't you sit down and have a cup of something while we discuss this calmly? Stay for supper if you like.' Mr Gwillim refused. 'I've got to open the Old People's concert in the town hall up at Williton at seven o'clock – though how many of them'll get there in this weather I don't know. Always the same. Work yourself to a shadow doing things for people and not a soul supports you.'

Bob tried to pacify Mr Gwillim, but the more reasonable he was, the angrier Mr Gwillim became. He was going to write to his Member of Parliament; he was going to write to the Town Council; he was going to write to the local newspaper; he was going to do everything possible to stop the railway from opening up again. Then he made for the door, but, unfortunately for him, Pest was on her way in, having escaped from her temporary paddock while Jessica's back was turned. The goat barged straight between Mr Gwillim's legs and toppled him into the fireplace. By the time Bob and Kathy had put him on his feet again and dusted him down, and Jessica and Jan had retrieved Pest, Mr Gwillim was white and trembling with fury. He stood by the door and said to Bob and the others, 'You're no better than gypsies – the lot of you

– and if I do nothing else I'm going to see the last of all of you in Flockton!' Then he stalked out into the fog-laden dusk.

Bob looked worried. He knew that Percy Gwillim had quite a lot of support from some of the more particular Flockton residents, and could well make it very difficult for the railway enthusiasts to start a scheduled service.

Jimmy came back from the Parcels Office. 'Are you expecting more visitors?' Bob looked out of the window; in the dim light of the station lamps he could see several muffled shapes making their way across the yard, led by Bill Jelly. Bob opened the door to invite them in, while Jan poked the fire into a fiercer warmth.

First Bill Jelly appeared, shivering and complaining about his rheumatism; behind him shuffled two men and a lady, all muffled to the eyes in scarves and overcoats. One of the men, very fat and bald and with a beard that made him look like a hairy balloon, went straight to the fire to warm his hands. His voice boomed when he spoke as though he were addressing a large assembly in a public hall. 'So sorry to intrude but we've lost our way in this damnable fog and saw your light ahead – perhaps you could put us on our way to Hardington?'

The Waiting Room was very crowded, with the Carter family observing the three strangers and Bill Jelly blowing his nose on a vast blue handkerchief. 'Found 'em goin' five miles an hour down the station approach in their Transit van. They'd've gone over the edge of the platform if I 'adn't stopped 'em.' The second man sniffed. He was young, very thin and pale, with bright ginger hair and he looked as though he'd been crying. The lady was unwrapping a seemingly endless woollen scarf from around her stringy neck while she cleared her throat like an old car starting up. The fat man introduced them. He himself was John Bromsgrove, a theatrical director and actor; the younger man was Izzy Finkle, who read his own poetry, and the tough old lady was Mrs Benbow, who played the piano and the drums.

They had all been on their way to give a recital of English folk art, 'Words and Music', to a select audience in Hardington. Jimmy thought they would have to be very select, if not selected, to get worked up about this lot – though he couldn't help feeling rather sorry for them. Mr Bromsgrove began braying an explanation. 'The fact is we are supposed to be at Hardington Public Library in one hour from now – and it looks to be impossible –

unless one of you good people could come with us, in our Transit van, to show us the way.' Izzy sobbed. 'The fog's got in my throat – I'll never be able to deliver properly.' 'Oh pull yourself together, you ninny!' Mrs Benbow barked at him.

Jan said, 'You'll never get there in an hour – not on a night like this – it's over fifteen miles away, on a terribly twisty road.' Jessica agreed. 'You'd only get there just as everybody was going home. Why don't you stay here and give us a turn instead?' Mr Bromsgrove swelled pinkly. 'A *turn*? We are not variety acts. We are . . .' he searched for the word, 'artistes.' He was about to go on indignantly, but Bob interrupted. 'How would you like to go by train? I've had steam up on the Flyer trying out the detonators – it's only twelve miles by rail and you can go faster along the track than by road – no oncoming traffic to look out for. I could get you there for seven-thirty.'

Mr Benbow nearly beamed and even Izzy brightened. 'Oh that would be lovely – you see my auntie lives in Taunton and she was coming specially to see me tonight.' They were all surprised and delighted to learn of the private railway line and full of thanks for the offer. Bob said it would take him only ten minutes to couple a carriage on and suggested that while they waited they could share the family supper. Then he slipped out with Jimmy to get the Flyer ready while steaming hot platefuls of Kathy's supper were quickly served to the visitors, Bill Jelly, and the family.

Bill looked at his unidentifiable mound of sauce in a bed of rice, sniffed it, put his ear to it, then tentatively nibbled a forkful. Mr Bromsgrove had beaten him to it and delivered a large spoonful into his wide mouth. At almost the same moment everyone else sampled it too and there was silence round the table, apart from the sound of heavy breathing and the odd whimper. Finally Bill said, 'Wot in the name of the Taj Mahal 'ave we got 'ere?' Tears were in Kathy's eyes as she replied, 'Curry. I'm afraid it is a bit hot. I upset the carton.' Izzy was gulping down a glass of water and Mrs Benbow was rolling a mouthful round her cheeks and whinnying. Jessica observed, between gasps for air, that it was a good thing to be warm inside when it was so cold out.

Bob and Jimmy returned just then with the news that all was ready for the journey to Hardington, and that they'd wait their supper till they got back. The three entertainers gathered themselves together, hurried outside, and loaded music stands, trunks and Mrs Benbow's drums from the Transit van on to the carriage linked behind the Flyer. Bob and Jimmy had mounted the foot-plate, and, as Bob set the engine in motion, Jimmy peered down the track ahead. A big bull's-eye lamp on the front of the engine showed through the fog for fifty yards ahead.

In the Waiting Room, Bill Jelly stretched himself lavishly in front of the fire and belched with vigour. 'This is the life . . . let them as wants gallivant about in fog with Hallowe'en pixies riskin' life and limb . . . give me a fire and a full belly and a good scratch. . . .' The last he at once proceeded to do, starting with his head, after taking off his hat, and then all over himself, with both hands. Jan came staggering in with a full coal-hod. She made the fire up and then turned to look at Bill, who had now scratched as far as his waist. 'It's always the same – men get to do the exciting stuff while women do the chores. I just wish I was out there battling through to Hardington against the clock.' Bill stopped in mid-massage. 'I don't. I wish I was sittin' by the fire with a full stomach and a nice cup o' tea. Now the only thing I ent got is the nice cup o' tea, 'ow about it?' Jan looked at the mangy old man with a mixture of pity and scorn. 'I'll get you one – but I think it's terrible not to have any spirit of adventure,' and she went into the Ticket Office.

The Flyer thudded determinedly along the track – Jimmy keeping the fire-box roaring, and, between shovelfuls, helping his father to keep a good look-out ahead. In the carriage behind, Mr Broms-grove, Mrs Benbow and Izzy peered through the windows into the dark sides of the cutting along which they were travelling. Mr Bromsgrove glanced at his fat, silver fob watch. 'Good time so far. I should think we're nearly halfway by now.' Izzy blew his nose. 'I've got a sore throat – I'll never be able to do justice to my poem about pollution.' Mrs Benbow laughed shrilly. 'Who do you think wants to hear it anyway? It's my drums they like – and my pianoforte solos.' Izzy sneered. 'Pity you can't manage them both at the same time, dear.' 'Now, now, my friends – no back-biting,' Mr Bromsgrove put in hastily. 'We're all in this together.' Just as he spoke there was a sudden terrific jolt and he was flung across the compartment into Mrs Benbow's lap. A case fell from the luggage rack and landed on Izzy's toe; he let out a wail.

The wheels screeched and skidded on the track as the Flyer wrenched to a halt with her dumb irons dug inches into the small hill of mud and boulders that filled the cutting. Bob released pressure and, as the shriek of steam subsided, turned and looked at Jimmy. 'That's that, then – a landslide – no chance of making Hardington now. Better get out and see how they fared in the rear; rather a sudden stop, I'm afraid.'

On the footplate Bob braked savagely. Jimmy had seen a great mound of earth and stones on the line ahead and yelled a warning. Bill Jelly put eight spoonfuls of sugar into the mug of tea Jan had brought him and stirred with care. Kathy and Jan had joined him by the fire while Jessica had gone back to Parcels to finish what Nuisance had left of her flower arrangement. Kathy was saying rather vaguely, 'I'm sure there are exciting jobs for girls too – imagine being a secretary to an oil tycoon, or somebody. You'd travel everywhere.' Jan wasn't convinced. 'Typing out other people's letters would be just as boring wherever you were doing it. I'm going to work for myself.'

At that moment the telephone jangled in the corner and Jan leaped to answer it. She recognized her father's voice and her heart jumped in case of an accident, but she was soon reassured as he told her of their near miss. He went on to say that he had decided to stop off at Lane End and telephone through to ask Kathy to get ready to put the Arts Council artistes up for the night, as there was nowhere they could go at such short notice. Bob added that all being well they should be back at Flockton in half an hour.

Jan gave her father's message to Kathy and they decided that if they handed the children's room over to their visitors, Jimmy could doss down on the sofa in the Waiting Room and Jan and Jessica would put up camp-beds in their parents' room. Bill grumbled, 'Just when you're settlin' in for a nice evenin's doze by the fire all 'ell breaks loose. I better get back to me kip in me 'ut.' He began to button up his various layers of garments as Kathy went through to warm the curry up again for Bob and Jimmy's return. Jan said unkindly, 'They'll be so hungry they might even eat it.' Kathy murmured, 'I don't know why I bother to try to give you all something different.' Then the telephone jangled again and once more Jan answered it.

Commander Frost's voice crackled through the ear piece. 'Frost here – emergency – callin' from Williton – Gwillim's made a muck as usual – the entertainers he ordered for the old folk ain't turned up. They're stranded in fog near Taunton and can't get through – thought you lot might help out – you know – sing-song – a few jokes – yer mother bangs the joanna don't she? Anything to keep the old folks amused.' Jan told the brusque old sailor that the Flyer was out on an emergency trip. Frost bawled down the telephone as though he was on the bridge of a ship in a full gale. 'Damn shame – don't know what we'll do then.'

That instant Jan had an idea. She looked at the old clock on the wall, which instead of twelve figures read 'G-R-E-A-T-W-E-S-T-E-R-N' all round – the old company that had once run the line. It showed R past E, or five past seven. She interrupted the Commander. 'Listen. Our emergency trip was to help some entertainers on their way to Hardington – not your sort – more arty – but I suppose they could do something – the funny lady's got drums at least – if I can get to the train in time to stop them at Williton you could still have a show tonight.' Commander Frost bellowed. 'Eh? What? How? Who?' But Janet shouted him down, 'No time to lose! Hold everything! Just trust me! You'll have a concert tonight – be sure of that!' and rang off.

Jessica had come through from the Parcels Office carrying Nuisance in one arm and a vase of autumn branches and leaves that looked like a hay stack which had been struck by lightning. 'Of course, the Japanese probably don't have cats to make things difficult.' Jan was already pulling on her boots by the door. 'I'm going to ride Trivet over the hill to Williton!' Bill protested: 'You ent got a saddle.' Jan said she'd do just as well bareback and grabbed her anorak from its peg.

Kathy poked her head through the hatch. 'Everything all right dear?' 'Fine – see you later – explain to her will you, Bill?' Jan shouted, and shot out of the door. Kathy looked at Bill inquiringly. Bill shrugged. 'She's gone 'untin', I think – for the train – so they can 'ave a concert.' Kathy blinked and Jessica complained. 'I found Trivet – I should have ridden him.' Bill said, 'You 'ave to be quick to get ahead of Jan.' Then he said good night quickly, in case anyone thought of asking him to do something energetic, and ambled out of the door into the blanketing fog. Kathy and Jessica looked at one another. Kathy said, 'Eccentricity's all very well – but sometimes I think all this family's completely round the bend.' Jessica argued, 'So long as we know we are it's not so bad' – and threw her Japanese flower arrangement on the fire, where it blazed brightly.

Jan kneed Trivet between trees, then, as they thinned out into rising heathland, she nudged him into a long Arabian trot.

Neither of them could see more than a yard or two ahead – but Jan knew every path and track between Flockton and Williton, and Trivet seemed to have complete trust in her firm hand on his rein and her sure knees guiding him round all obstacles. As she rode, Jan willed Trivet to get there in time to stop the Flyer and save the old people from disappointment.

Mr Bromsgrove and his two companions had sorted themselves out again for the return journey. Izzy had taken his shoe off and was trying to kiss his toe better. They were all shaken and a little fearful, for now they were being pushed down the line backwards – though Jimmy was in the end compartment stuck halfway out of the window, with the bull's-eye lamp in one hand showing the way, and a white handkerchief in the other to wave to his father in the engine behind if he should meet any obstacle. Mrs Benbow complained stridently, 'I knew we shouldn't have set out tonight – it was all your fault, Brommy.' Mr Bromsgrove told her firmly, 'The show must go on – you know that as well as I do.' He imagined she must feel the same as he did – terribly let down. 'When you're all ready to do a show and something happens to stop you – such an anticlimax.' Izzy wailed, 'I don't care if I never have to do another show – so long as I get back safe to somewhere warm.'

There were a good many bends between Bishop's Lydeard and Williton, so Bob had to go slowly. His eyes watered from staring along the carriage to look for Jimmy's warning handkerchief. Bob reckoned they must be nearly at Williton Station by now – then it would be a nice straight run most of the way back to Flockton. Sure enough, the black shapes of the station buildings showed up in the dark, and the sound of the train echoed back. Bob could just make out the sign 'Williton Station'. Then he thought he must be imagining things. A horse and rider were trotting along the platform beside him. Just before the end of the platform he recognized Jan, signalling frantically, and once again he braked hard. In the carriage, once again, Mr Bromsgrove, Izzy and Mrs Benbow were rolled in a heap among their fallen cases – shrieking pathetically.

At Williton Town Hall over a hundred old people – members of the Senior Citizens Club – were gathered, waiting patiently and expectantly for the entertainment to commence. On the stage behind the curtain, Commander Frost and Percy Gwillim were engaged in high words, both blaming each other for the break-down in organization. Mr Gwillim was just about to announce cancellation and tell everyone to go home – in spite of Commander Frost's protests that a stand-by troupe were on the way and due at any moment. Mr Gwillim grasped the curtains to make his way to the front of the stage. The Commander called, 'Heave to!' A harassed Mr Bromsgrove was shepherding his two companions from the wings, followed by Jan Carter.

Mr Bromsgrove had been briefed about his audience on his way from Williton Station, and was making quick adjustments to his programme to accommodate them. As Jimmy and Bob carried in Mrs Benbow's drums and their stage clothes, Mr Bromsgrove swept off his overcoat. 'We'll start with Mrs Benbow's Indian tom-tom act – then Izzy – you can do your Cyril Fletcher imitation – I shall follow with Sergeant Buzfuz from the *Pickwick Papers* – then Mrs Benbow can lead community songs on the piano. From there on we'll play it by ear!'

The concert was a riotous success. Even Percy Gwillim was forced in the end to admit that the Carter family had saved the day – or rather the night, though he wouldn't accept an invitation to go back to Flockton Station to sample some of Kathy's curry – which was perhaps just as well.

Towards midnight, with a blazing fire in the Waiting Room, and hot drinks dispelling the gloom outside, the Arts Council artistes and the Carters were loud in praise of each other's quick wit and initiative. And Trivet, snug in his stable, blew round the bin containing the last of a bran mash laced with Guinness, and wondered, perhaps, at the strange ways of humans, who wanted him to charge across country on a foggy night just to say hello to a legless iron horse that sneezed all the time – and then come home again.

CHAPTER 4
CHRISTMAS SPECIAL

In the Parcels Office a paraffin stove gave out a cosy warmth. Outside, snow congealed on the panes of the windows and flickered past them like an old-fashioned kaleidoscope. It was Sunday morning, with two weeks of school left before the Christmas holidays. Jan was pulling on a heavy jersey, getting ready to go out. Jimmy was squatting on his bed trying to make out a list of Christmas presents for the family.

He had made a picture frame to contain a large colour photograph of the Flyer. A schoolmate whose father was a photographer had had it blown up for him. That took care of Dad. Jimmy had also bought two lovely leather-bound volumes of Rudyard Kipling, at a second-hand shop in Hardington. They had been a bit mildewy, so he had got them cheap, but he had cleaned them up and polished the covers till they gleamed an invitation to look inside. They were for Kathy. That left Jan, Jess, Bill and the Commander. Jack Frost had given the youngsters book tokens for the last three Christmases.

Jimmy looked out of the window. He could see Jessica in the middle distance, carrying a huge armful of hay across the yard. She passed their father and Bill Jelly, tinkering with a contraption on the front of the Flyer. Jimmy was baffled for a moment – then he grinned as he realized what it was. A snow-plough. 'Dad's being a bit pessimistic, isn't he?' Jan shrugged on her duffel coat. 'Why?' 'D'you think we'll get enough snow to need a snow-plough on the Flyer?' Jan looked out of the window. 'You never know. If it kept up like this for a day or two we might easily be cut right off. That'd be rather fun, wouldn't it?' Jimmy wasn't sure. What would Jessica say if they had to start eating the animals? Jan smiled as she took up a saddle and bridle and wiped them over with a damp rag.

Across the yard, Jessica pushed her way into the disused coal bunker which had been rigged up as a pen for Pest. The gentle little goat came out from her lean-to hut, bleating an affectionate and greedy greeting. Jessica pushed the hay inside the hut, out of the falling snow, and Pest followed it back in and started tucking into the mound of sweet-smelling memories of summer. Jessica patted her head and went out, carefully snibbing the gate behind her. Then she picked up a bucket of corn and carried it to the wired-off piece of scratched turf where their eight hens and Dick Duck appeared to be jumping up and down in the snow to keep warm. Dick Duck, a brightly coloured muscovy, had been a present from a local farmer who they'd helped out in the summer. Jessica scattered the corn and picked five eggs out of the back of the coop. Not too bad for the time of year. Next spring Bob had promised to get a cockerel to fertilize the eggs so that they could hatch out some chicks.

Jessica carried the eggs and bucket back across the yard to the station buildings. She had fed Trivet an hour before to give him time to digest before she and Jan took him out for a ride. Nuisance the cat had finished her breakfast and was sitting under a window-ledge trying to catch snowflakes on her tongue. That's everyone fed till tea-time, thought Jessica, as she kicked the snow from her boots and went inside.

Kathy was tidying up in the Ticket Office as she listened to yet another recipe on Radio Two. Jessica asked if there was anything she could do before she went out. Kathy shook her head as music took the place of the disc jockey's manic tones. 'That recipe was for a Christmas turkey.' Kathy sighed. 'I don't think the jam-jar will run to one, though.' They kept all their ready cash in a jam-jar in the old wall safe with the butter, milk, bacon and other perishables. She looked at Jessica. 'Do you think we could make do with one of the hens?' Jessica looked a bit shaken. 'Do we have to choose which one?' Kathy said no, Bob would do that, and they'd never remember which it was. Jessica objected, 'I would – I know each one – it'd be like eating a friend – I couldn't possibly. It's like being a cannibal.' Kathy looked sympathetic. 'It was just a thought. We'll try and dream up something else.' Jan came through, carrying the saddle and bridle, and said, 'Ready to tack up?' She and Jessica went out together to one of the old engine sheds which Jimmy had blocked off to make a stable for Trivet.

Across the yard, Bill Jelly blew on his fingers and stamped his feet as he watched Bob tighten a bolt on the great iron contraption they had fashioned from two old fire-grates, bits of rail, and a corrugated-iron water-butt. It looked as if it would clear snow from the front of the Flyer all right, but you couldn't tell till you saw it in action, which is what they were about to try. Bob looked up. 'Hey, Bill – we haven't got a snowdrift to try it on. Can you pile some up in front and we'll see how it works?' Bill muttered to himself. 'Any 'ard labour – that's me – no one understands – I ent got long,' but he took a long-handled shovel and started piling snow, ten yards up the track ahead of the Flyer.

Jimmy strolled over and watched him interestedly. 'Have you ever thought, Bill,' he said, 'that there are some people who are cut out for doing, and some for thinking? I think you're one of the doers.' Bill said, 'Get lost!' and Jimmy moved to the footplate where his father was throwing coal in the fire-box. 'How goes it, Dad?' Bob looked down, sweating in spite of the cold. 'OK so far. Only one problem. We have to think of some way of keeping the Flyer in the public eye between now and the Grand Opening next spring. Jack Frost says the Society members will get restive otherwise. Huh! I wouldn't mind if they got a bit restive helping out here from time to time.' Jimmy thought for three seconds. 'How about a Santa Claus Special?' Bob stopped chucking coal about and wiped sweat from his eyes as he looked down questioningly. Jimmy went on, 'Kids. Little kids. Get 'em on the Flyer at Flockton – mums and dads with them. Run up the line to Lane End. At Lane End Father Christmas is waiting. Gives them all a toy out of his sack. Then chuff them all back.'

Bob was flabbergasted. He wondered again how he had managed to father such a brilliant son. One pound for the return journey, including the toy. And there was a lot of spare lumber out at the back; if they all got down to making wooden engines, ducks on wheels and hobby-horses, the toys could cost very little. They could make several hundred pounds with any luck and the toys

43

might be far nicer than a lot of things people bought in the shops these days. He said, 'You're on! Jimmy – you and Jan organize the toy end and I'll work out the schedules.' Jimmy thought they'd got the hard end of the bargain as usual. Why didn't he keep his mouth shut? Still, if the girls and Basil Humpthorn and Geoff Gosling would help they should be able to turn out enough in the next week or two to fill a few sacks. They could all do the painting. There were about ten gallons of red and blue paint – plus a little gold – left over from the carriage renovations.

Jan and Jessica crossed the yard bound for the wide open spaces of the Quantocks. Jessica was travelling pillion behind Jan and the stocky little horse appeared to bear them both with ease. Of course, when the going got rough Jan would get off and trudge alongside. Bob called, 'Not too far! This snow looks as though it's going to keep up for a while yet – it could make getting back difficult.' Jan waved in acknowledgement and Trivet ambled silently up the track towards the hills, his hooves muffled in the snow. Bob shouted, 'All right Bill?'

Bill gave a 'thumbs-up' sign. Bob eased the Flyer forward; as she approached the six-foot pile of snow Bill had created, the makeshift snow-plough dug in and with a smooth cut turned the pile of snow to one side, enabling the Flyer to steam past it up the track. Bob yelled with delight, shut off power, and leaped down to join Jimmy and Bill. Clasping hands, the trio did a little dance under the falling snow, back across the yard to the buildings, leaving tracks behind them like a herd of stampeding cattle, and disappeared inside for a cup of hot something.

Jan and Jessica made their way up a steep track to the crest of Hangman's Hill. Jessica was in the saddle now, with Jan ploughing through the deep snow beside her, hanging on to the left stirrup. A thousand feet above the sea they stopped by the ancient beacon point that had been used to burn warning fires in case of invaders. They looked about them. The snow had ceased for a while, and a great silence was folded between the sea and land and grey sky; wide white icing lay over the folds of the land below them like a giant's birthday cake, the green candles of trees counting an ageless celebration.

To their right a long slope up ended in a sharp fall of rock, dropping a hundred feet to a small sheltered ingle. The two girls breathed in the crisp salt air and relished the quiet. In a moment it was broken by a panic bleating from the far crevice. Jessica said, 'I'll see what's up! – you follow!' She dug her heels into Trivet's flanks, sending him leaping through two foot of snow like a demented hare, Jan plunging behind as best she could. Panting, she yelled, 'Mind the edge!' and then staggered on, knee deep.

In the snug of the Exciseman, Bob Carter and Commander Frost faced a purple-cheeked Percy Gwillim. He was purple partly from cold, partly from temper and partly from port. Bob had gone down to the pub in answer to an alarm call from the Commander who was, as he put it, 'feelin' a bit outgunned'.

Gwillim was pressing ahead with his plans to prevent the opening of the first scheduled public service of the line in the coming spring. He had got as far as persuading the Department of the Environment to hold a public enquiry on the issue in March of the new year. Apparently he had been brought to the boil that day by 'offensive noise levels' the evening before. While Bob had been down at Lane End fixing some points, Basil Humpthorn and Geoff Gosling with a few other helpers had allowed their enthusiasm to outdistance their sense of time and had been laying some track for an extra siding by floodlight until nearly eight o'clock, when the snow had started. Unfortunately the new siding lay just beneath Percy Gwillim's house.

Bob took a sup of beer, and told the irate gentleman that it would not happen again; this succeeded in calming him down a little. Then Bob, whose own enthusiasm was often too great to be contained for long, blurted out to the Commander Jimmy's plan for a Santa Claus Special. Percy Gwillim swallowed like a giraffe and then really hit the rafters. Couldn't he even enjoy the season of goodwill uninterrupted by the hated engine? Wasn't it supposed to be a time of peace on earth? What chance of peace with the Flyer thumping up and down all day? Commander Frost said, 'But what about the little kiddies? Think of their smilin' faces – bless their hearts – with Santa meeting them off the train.' Mr Gwillim banged down his glass and, with his face set in harsh lines of fury, left the snug, nearly colliding with Bill Jelly who was on his way in for 'a quick snifter'.

Commander Frost went to the bar to get a round in for the three of them, while Bob filled Bill in about the Santa Claus Special. Bill was enchanted. ''Ere – you got an experienced Santa on yer very threshold – I bin Father Christmas all over the world. London stores, New York stores, and once even in Australia when it was 'ot as porridge – it bein' summer at the time like what it is in the Anti Podes.'

Commander Frost came back from the bar with their beer. 'I've been thinkin', Carter – I'd make rather a good Santa meself – once played Father Neptune crossin' the date line – damn good show that – always wanted to be Santa, though – watch the little smilin' rosy faces light up. . . .' His eyes were moist with longing. Bob glanced from him to Bill Jelly, who was beginning to glower jealously. 'Oh dear,' thought Bob, 'even this idea is going to be complicated by crusty rivalry.'

Jan, Jessica and Trivet stood some yards from the edge of the steep slope, looking down. The high drop had shielded the little cleft below from the worst of the snow. Here a dozen sheep had gathered, to escape the wind and nibble at the bare green grass that had been left uncovered. Unfortunately, having slithered down there, the silly creatures seemed unable to find their way up again, and the other end of the cleft ended in another, almost sheer, drop, which formed part of a cutting to the single-line railway track that lay below, running between Flockton and Lane End. The moment they saw the horse and the humans looking down on them, the sheep redoubled their frantic baa-aaing. Jessica looked at Jan. 'D'you think if they get more panicky they might try to climb out and fall down and hurt themselves? Or even break their necks?'

Jan thought privately that sheep were probably silly enough to do anything, but she didn't want to add to Jessica's distress. 'I tell you what. I'll scramble down there and try and keep them calm while you ride Trivet back to Flockton and get Dad to bring the Flyer up here. We'll find some way of getting them to safety, and then Dad can take them back in a truck. I wonder whose they are? Never mind – off you go!' Jessica led Trivet farther back from the brink, got in the saddle, and urged him on down the way they had come. After looking to see that her sister was managing,

Jan looked down for footholds, then eased herself over the edge as the sheep baaed more frantically than ever.

Jessica urged Trivet down a rutted track as quickly as was safe. As they rounded a corner, she heard rending, slithering sounds ahead, and then saw a Land-Rover half on the track and half in a ditch. As she got closer she recognized the furious face of Mr Gwillim in the driving seat. The snow was starting to fall again, and as he raced the engine the wheels could get no grip on the slippery ground. Although he was no friend of her family, Jessica felt bound to offer some sort of assistance. 'Is there anything we can do?' Mr Gwillim glowered. 'I doubt it. I've lost some sheep and was going back to look for them – the worst thing is, my dog's got a split paw, so I'm on my own.' Jessica quickly told him what she and Jan had discovered and then she noticed a coil of rope in the truck. 'D'you think that if Trivet and I gave you an extra little heave when you run the engine you might pull out?'

Mr Gwillim nodded morosely. He hated to be seen at a disadvantage. He tied one end of the rope to the front bumper and Jessica made a rope harness at the other end which she fixed on Trivet. Mr Gwillim broke off some branches from the hedge and put them in front of the wheels, then he got in. . . . Jessica led Trivet up the track until the rope was taut, then, as the engine roared into gear, she coaxed Trivet to heave on the rope. For a moment nothing happened, then suddenly the wheels gripped on the branches and the Land-Rover lurched forward and back on to the track. Jessica took the harness off Trivet and got in the saddle again. 'If you carry on for about a mile you'll see the cliff where they are – just under Hangman's Hill. Can you keep Jan company there till I get back home? I'm going to ask Dad to bring the Flyer out.' Mr Gwillim finished coiling the rope. 'I'll manage all right – no need to go to all that trouble.' Jessica thought, 'Pig-headed old donkey,' but out loud she said, 'You'll never get to the sheep from this end. Much better to lower them down to the railway track.' Mr Gwillim thought it over. He might have been an idiot – but he wasn't a fool. 'All right,' he said, 'I'll go on and mind your sister till that Flyer thing gets here. And ask your father to hurry. The snow's getting worse.' And he started to drive the Land-Rover up the track.

He was right about the snow. Jessica could see less than fifty yards ahead through the thick flakes – but she was fairly certain of her way. She wasn't sure Jan would be exactly happy having Percy Gwillim for company, but it would be better than being left entirely on her own. Trivet trudged over a hump-backed bridge and Jessica gave a sigh of relief as she recognized it as being quite near Flockton Station.

The fire roared in the Waiting Room; Clancy ruffled his feathers luxuriously in the warmth and squawked, 'Oh to be in England now that April's there', or something like that. Kathy said automatically, 'Quiet Clancy,' and continued taking her history notes. She had an exam after Christmas and had got a bit behind with her studies. Jimmy had reckoned up the wood and paint that were available, and was working out how many toys they would turn out.

Bob was estimating times of arrival and departure for the Santa Claus Special and Bill Jelly was squatting by the fire sipping one of his special mugs of tea, half full of sugar. 'I'm the obvious choice for Santa,' he grumbled, 'I've 'ad expert experience. That old pirate don't know nuffin' about it. Scare the kids to death he would – shoutin' at 'em.' Jimmy said, 'So long as you're there to scare them back to life . . .' Bob interrupted hastily, 'Jim's jokes,' and went on. 'We'll decide later. If necessary we'll toss for it.' He remembered Jack Frost's last words to him, spoken in a whisper that had wobbled the cobwebs among the beams of the Exciseman. 'If you give Father Christmas to that scruffy old vagabond – well – I'll say no more except stormy seas ahead . . . I mean look at me, dammit – did you ever see such a natural Santa? Y'need someone . . .' he had to search for the word, '. . . benign.'

Jimmy heard a muffled clumping in the yard just as Kathy said, 'I'd better get something on the go – I should think Jan and Jess will have worked up quite an appetite.' Jimmy opened the yard door just as Jessica looped Trivet's reins round the old station lamp post and ran over. She burst past Jimmy into the Waiting Room, crying breathlessly, 'Dad! Everyone! You'll have to get the Flyer out fast up to Hangman's Hill. There's some sheep caught there and Jan's with them.' The family wasted no time. Bob, Kathy and Jimmy were getting their coats and boots on while Jessica filled them in on the whole story. Bill, fully dressed as always – they had never seen him take any part of his clothes off –

went straight out to get the box truck ready to couple on the Flyer. By the time Bob had raised enough steam to start, and Jessica had quickly led Trivet into his warm stable and rugged him, everyone else was on the truck ready to go. Jessica pushed the points over to the main line and swung aboard as the Flyer clanked slowly past.

At first the snow-plough appeared to be unnecessary, but as the track wound out on to the more exposed reaches of the coastline, the drifts of snow got worse, blown up against the landward cliffs. The plough worked well, scything a way through, but, even so, their progress was slow. Kathy, Jess and Bill, in the truck, were feeling fairly frozen when a double toot on the whistle told them they were approaching the cutting under Hangman's Hill.

Bill slid the door back on its rollers, and, as the engine slowed, they all looked out and up and could see Jan and Mr Gwillim waving from the cliff top above. Bob organized everyone quickly and efficiently. Jimmy started to climb up with one end of a long rope and a pair of makeshift tarpaulin harnesses for each sheep to be strapped in one at a time. Jan started down the cliff, took the rope's end from Jimmy and threw it up to Mr Gwillim, who wound it, firmly knotted, round a boulder. Then, rejoined by Jan, he bound the first struggling baa-aaing sheep firmly in the bo'sun's chair and hooked it on to the rope. Lacking a block and tackle, they were unable to adjust the speed of the sheep's descent; so Kathy, Jimmy and Bill were strung out up the steep slope to try and grab the creature as it whizzed past, to slow it up a little. The last few yards of rope curved up towards the roof of the truck where Bob stood to catch it.

All went well till by the fifth sheep everyone had got a bit over-confident. . . . Jan gave it a shove to start it off on its improvised ski-lift journey and slipped and fell head first into a huge snow-drift. After the push the animal was travelling so fast that everyone who attempted to grab at it was yanked off their feet to flounder likewise. Bob standing his ground, caught the flying quadruped full tilt in his stomach and disappeared over the back of the truck's roof. They all picked themselves up, not too much the worse for wear, and from then on went more carefully.

At last all twelve of the sheep were safely in the box truck, where the humans huddled among them to stay warm after their exertions. Mr Gwillim stood on the footplate with Bob and Jimmy

to keep an eye out for the fold on lower ground where he wanted to drop the sheep off. Father and son both noticed he seemed to have difficulty in keeping his face in lines of displeasure. The Flyer stopped near his farm, and two men came out to help him tease the flock into the fold. Just before the Flyer left, Percy Gwillim turned back and called out, 'Won't give you any trouble over the Christmas Special – thanks for your help.' Bob shouted, 'That's very big of you, Mr Gwillim.' Then the farmer added, 'Still haven't changed my mind long term, though. Public inquiry in March still stands.' And he stalked off towards the farm buildings. Bob gave a derisive toot on the whistle as the Flyer rumbled off, and Mr Gwillim, turning back, missed his footing and disappeared from sight into a snow-filled hollow, only the jerking heels of his boots showing as the Flyer puffed round the bend.

Commander Frost was waiting for them in the Waiting Room when they all got back, soaked and raw and cold. As people trundled to and fro, changing into dry clothes, putting kettles on, making the fire up and preparing food, Jack Frost mumbled on about 'the Christmas Special failing dismally without his personal fantastic appearance as Santa', to anyone in hearing range. With the exception of Bill Jelly, that is. Whenever their eyes met they both looked away, sulking and smouldering with resentment. At last Kathy brought through an enormous pan of Sahara stew – 'It's supposed to be made out of camels' bones and sour goats' milk, but I had to make do with gravy cubes and Pest's fresh milk with a few other things I found lying about.' Whatever the other things had been, they certainly seemed to have turned the scales in the stew's favour – and flavour – for everyone pronounced it excellent.

As they were digesting it, in an uncomfortable silence brought about by snide asides addressed across the table by Commander Frost and Bill Jelly, concerning their rival abilities in impersonating old men with long white beards, Jimmy suddenly yelped with glee. 'Of course! Stupid nit I am, not to have thought of it before.' The rest looked questioning. 'One at either end! Don't you see? One Santa sees the children off at Flockton and the other welcomes them at Lane End!!' Kathy said, 'But won't the children wonder why there are two Father Christmases?' Jimmy shook his head. 'Not at all – it'll add to the magic. We can tell them that

Santa flies through the sky faster than the train and gets there before them.' At first Bill and Jack Frost weren't too happy at sharing the honours, but at the same time each was so worried about being left out that they consented.

So it happened that two weeks later, two weeks that had been spent in a riot of activity, making toys and painting them, decorating the Flyer with pine branches and holly, making two identical costumes for Santa Claus and filling the sacks ready for presentation, the first group of little children with their parents gathered at Number One Platform at Flockton Station and were seen off by a white whiskered Commander Frost, roaring with jolly laughter and blowing his whistle fit to bust. And at Lane End they were met off the train by a white-whiskered Bill Jelly, sitting gingerly on the horse Trivet, who sported a set of antlers bound behind his ears, neither apparently any the worse for going a hundred miles an hour through the sky to get to Lane End before the Flyer and greet the little ones with a full sack of presents after their journey up the line.

The Flyer made two trips a day for ten days and all the villages around thought it was a marvellous idea. On Christmas Day, as the Carters and their two Santas sat around replete, after eating a huge turkey sent down from Mr Gwillim in thanks for their help with his sheep, everyone felt most optimistic about the year ahead and the growing affection of the people of the Quantock valley for their great, grand, green-and-gold, gorgeous mascot, the famous Flockton Flyer.

CHAPTER 5
ANCHORS AWEIGH!

The small, bright blue boat sat quite still in gleaming black water that barely rippled. Jimmy sensed a jerk on his rod. He called to Jan, who had been dreaming shorewards, and she scrambled forrard with the landing net. Jimmy reeled in, and Jan caught the fish neatly and brought it inboard. A fine plaice. 'About three pounds I guess,' said Jimmy, and looked down at the other plaice and two dab that lay in the bottom of the boat.

Jan gazed towards the shore again as she stowed the net. A cabin cruiser was put-put-putting out from Flockton Wall, cutting a clear wake through oily sullen sea. 'Isn't that Basil's boat?' Jimmy looked, and nodded. 'Wonder what he's coming out for?' The far horizon was like a thick black pencil line and the sky was leaden. 'We'd better get back. It's too calm for my liking – something's going to explode soon.' Jimmy took up one oar and Jan the other, and they started to pull for the shore.

The boat belonged to Geoff Gosling, who had lent it to them for an afternoon's fishing. His cottage showed yellow on the cliff, nestling above two black mouths of caves that gaped over the little bay Jimmy and Jan were headed for. Between grunts Jan said, 'D'you think there are any smugglers about here still?' Jimmy jerked out, 'No. Only people you get in those caves now are snugglers.' Jan giggled. Occasionally Jim's jokes were quite funny.

Basil Humpthorn's cruiser *Helen* was coming up on them fast and they could hear him hailing them. 'Heave to, will you?' He cut his motor and turned in a sure swathe to come alongside. He smiled down. 'I saw you were out here and thought you might appreciate a tow in. The tide's on the turn and I don't like the look of that sky . . . the old calm before the storm. Come aboard.' Jimmy threw him the painter which Basil made fast to the stern. *Helen* was a neat boat, twenty-seven foot, with sails as well as the engine. As Basil prepared to start up again, Jimmy said, 'I s'pose we couldn't sail back. It's much more fun.'

Basil took stock. There was a slight ruffle now on the surface of the sea and a halyard fidgeted against the mast in a slight breeze. Should be enough. He smiled at Jimmy and Jan's eager faces, and on his commands they quickly made sail. This wasn't the first time they'd been on board with him and they were already becoming quite adept. He kept the bows into the wind as best he could, and as Jimmy hauled the mainsail aloft it filled slowly in the freshening breeze and Basil allowed *Helen* to veer round towards the shore. There was a distant rumble of thunder. Basil said, 'Just as well to sail – there's very little petrol in the tank. D'you mind if we anchor by Geoff's? He's going to take me over to Taunton this afternoon to get a few final signatures for the public enquiry tonight.' Jan and Jimmy didn't mind. They thought they'd look in on Bill at his hut on the way home, and take him one of their fish. Far up the coast puffs of white smoke showed against the darkening sky. The Flyer was returning from Lane End. 'Do you think we'll win tonight, Basil?' asked Jan.

Her father and Commander Frost had been up to Lane End seeking last-minute support for keeping the line open. The inquiry at Flockton Town Hall that night at seven o'clock would decide things one way or another. Basil stopped humming a sea shanty. 'Difficult to say. Old Gwillim's certainly been doing his best to get us stopped. Depends on . . . that's odd.' He broke off.

Jimmy and Jan looked where his finger was pointing. The distant green insect that was the Flyer had stopped. As they watched, the puffs of smoke started again, but the train was going back on itself. Jimmy grimaced. 'The Commander's sure to have left something important behind – he always does. I can't imagine how he ever managed to command a ship – he's so absent-minded.' The wind died momentarily and the boat, with the smaller dinghy bobbing listlessly at her stern, lost way, and began to drift

with the tide. They weren't worried. No one was in any great
hurry. . . .

On the footplate of the Flyer, Bob and Commander Frost regarded the huge man who was squeezed between them and the
tender. He was bigger than the two of them put together, with a
cropped head like a stone gate ornament and arms and legs like
an erect cart-horse. Bob took a quick look out of the cab for
clearance ahead. 'About another two miles to Crowcombe Rocks.
How badly hurt is your friend?' The giant growled in a deep
Welsh rumble. 'Broken leg, I think. His own damn silly fault for
not lookin' where he was goin', wasn't it?' Jack Frost tut-tutted.
'Don't you worry, though – we'll have him safe and sound in a
trice. Don't mind my sayin' so – funny time of year for bird-
watchin?' The man grinned, showing half his teeth were missing.
'We're very enthusiastic, though, see?'

Bob glanced back in the cab. He didn't think the man looked
like an ornithologist. Surely he'd be carrying binoculars or something. Still, you never could tell. They were approaching a slight
gradient and Bob released more power.

Basil Humpthorn eased *Helen* into the small rocky inlet and called
to Jimmy and Jan to drop anchor. As they did so, he let down the
mainsail and the boat veered stern on to the shore with the incom-
ing tide. Basil put down a storm anchor aft; he didn't like the
look of the sky at all. They piled into the smaller boat and rowed
the few yards to the sand-spit; once ashore, they pulled it high up,
well above high-water mark. Then they crossed the railway line
and Basil started to make his way up the path to Geoff's cottage,
while Jimmy and Jan walked along the track towards the plate-
layers' hut.

As they got near, they could see Bill Jelly outside taking a
ruined pair of long woollen underpants off a makeshift clothes
line. Jimmy and Jan looked at each other, amazed. They'd never
realized Bill ever washed anything. Then he turned and saw them
and quickly hid the underwear beneath his coats and scuttled
inside the hut. 'Pretend we haven't seen,' muttered Jimmy. 'He's
obviously embarrassed.' Bill was opening the door as they came up,

56

grinning cheerily. 'Nice to see you. Bin fishin', eh? Come in and 'ave a cuppa – I got the kettle on.'

It was very cosy, with the wind beginning to whine outside. One window looked up the line, and another had a view across Blue Anchor Bay, now grey and angry-looking. Jan and Jimmy moved close to the iron stove, glowing under a hissing kettle.

As Bill turned from getting two more tin mugs off a shelf, Jimmy did one of his lightning mimes. He traced a question mark in the air, flapped his elbows and scratched with one foot, then peered, long-necked, into the distance. Bill was ready for the test, 'Why did the chicken cross the road?' Then he grinned slyly as he put his hands to his ears and wiggled them, lolloped across the room as though on four legs, stood erect, and drew straight lines in the air. Jimmy looked at Jan, somewhat put out. 'You got me there, Bill.' Bill cackled, ''Cos it saw the zebra crossin','' and took down a bag of sugar and a tin of milk. Jan said, 'If we can wait here till the Flyer comes back through, we can get a lift home to Flockton. It should have been through by now, but we saw it go back up the line – so it may be another half-hour.' 'Relax and enjoy yerselves,' Bill insisted. 'You're better off inside while this storm's brewin'.'

The Flyer stood hissing by another hut five miles up the line at Crowcombe Rocks. The Commander and Bob had had no chance. As they'd got off the Flyer, the giant had sprung on the Commander without warning and twisted his arm behind him. Then he had threatened Bob that if he didn't do what he was told the Commander would get a broken arm; and by the crazy glint in his eye Bob knew he meant it.

Commander Frost was apoplectic. 'What the blue starin' blazes d'you think you're up to?' The Welsh giant had the old sailor in a grip of iron, one arm round his throat and the other pinning him helpless. The giant hissed in his ear, 'Keep quiet, you old fool, and you might not get hurt – see?' Jack Frost turned his popping eyes to the hut as Bob came from it, helping a youth who was yelping in agony. He was supported on the other side by a young woman with long tawny hair. Bob grimaced helplessly at the Commander as the giant shouted, 'Lay him in that truck now and then get back on this engine – and be quick about it! You

stay with him, Bridget, and keep his mind off his hurt – try singin'
"Men of Harlech" – that should buck him up no end.' He laughed
coarsely and yanked Commander Frost off his feet and towards
the footplate.

Bob laid the youth gently in the truck and Bridget took off a
suède jacket and laid it under his head. His injured leg was bound
in a rough splint with a broken branch and some strips torn from
his shirt sleeve. Bob looked at Bridget. 'How do you come to be
mixed up in this mess? What's going on?'

Bridget was muttering, 'We didn't know it was going to be like
this – Ewan and me. Big Hughie said it was going to be a bit of a
prank. You see – the Organization was very angry about the reser-
voirs taking all the water from Wales to England during the
drought. Hughie said he wanted us to help him open all the stop-
cocks on the great reservoir above Hardington. But then Ewan
and I – we're engaged, see – we found Big Hughie was going to
use dynamite, so we decided to lose him. We were on motor-
bikes and Hughie chased us to these rocks and Ewan skidded and
broke his leg. I don't know what's happening now.'

Bob spun round as he heard a cry of pain from the Commander
and a loud bellow from Big Hughie. 'Hurry yourselves up there!'
Bob said quickly, 'I must go – I'll do what I can to help,' and
jumped down from the truck, along to the Flyer and up on to the
footplate. Big Hughie had the Commander pressed against the
tender. 'Now take us along the coast to where we can get a boat.'
Bob eased the regulator over. 'Boat?' Big Hughie nodded. 'Take
us back across the Bristol Channel to the Mumbles light – there's
plenty lonely places along there where we can land. Your police
will be watchin' the roads but they won't be lookin' for a boat,
will they?'

Bob said, 'I'm surprised you haven't run off on your own and
left your two friends to face the music.' 'Ah, well, see – Ewan is
my sister Gwynneth's lad and she'd give me hell if anything
happened to him. She'll give me hell as it is – but not so much as
if he got put in jail.' The giant looked almost tearful as he added,
'My sister Gwynneth's only four foot ten but she makes up for it
by havin' a tongue a yard long. . . .' Bob thought, 'We've got a
right nutter here – have to watch our step.'

Bob put his head out of the cab to stare along the line. The
track ran right down the valley only minutes, now, from the coast.

A spot of rain stung his face and he noticed some gulls wheeling in from a dark horizon. 'Deserve all they get if they put to sea in this,' he thought, but he couldn't help feeling sorry for the lad Ewan.

In the hut the old tramp took out his fob watch. 'Takin' their time comin' back, ent they?' Jimmy nodded. 'I dunno what's kept them. If they're not here in five minutes we'd better start walking.' A squall of rain spattered the seaward window and Bill cackled, 'Better you nor me.' Jan said, 'Perhaps we could leave the fish and the tackle here – save carrying them. Have what you want for your tea.' Bill thanked her. 'Just fancy a nice bit of fish . . .' Jimmy held up his hands. 'Sssh! Listen!' Over the gusts of wind they could hear quite distinctly the nearby panting of the Flyer. 'Come on – quick!' said Jimmy, and dashed outside, followed by Jan.

Big Hughie glared from the cab, still keeping a tight hold on poor Commander Frost, who was beginning to wilt a bit under the strain. The giant saw two things simultaneously. First, the two youngsters running from the hut, signalling to stop; the second, the cruiser *Helen* rolling in the broken waves of the inlet, a few hundred yards down from the track. Although big, Hughie was not slow-witted. 'Brake!' he shouted. Bob disregarded him. He wasn't going to risk Jimmy and Jan anywhere near this madman. Then, hearing a shout of terror, he looked round. Big Hughie had pushed Jack Frost more than halfway out of the cab. 'You brake – or I'll drop him – and he'll break!!' Bob knew he meant it and was powerless. He braked violently and saw the Commander jerked back into the cab.

Jimmy and Jan had seen the Commander pop in and out like a sideways Jack-in-the-box, and stopped short, feeling a bit panicky. Then the Flyer halted level with them and they saw the strange group in the cab. Bob called down, 'Get lost! Get back home! Run all the way' – but Big Hughie shouted him down. 'If you know what's good for this old boy you'll stay where you are.' Then he eased himself down from the cab, pulling the Commander after him like a broken puppet. Bridget peered anxiously from the truck behind. Big Hughie called to her. 'Stay where you are for now – the rest of you into that hut – double quick!'

Bill Jelly had certainly never entertained such a strange party in his life. Big Hughie grasped a steaming mug of tea in one hand and retained a firm grasp on the Commander with the other, while the rest looked on helplessly. The giant gulped from his mug and spoke harshly, 'Now here's what we're goin' to do, see? Me and this old feller is goin' to get on that motor cruiser down there and you two youngsters is comin' too.' As Bob started to protest, 'That'll stop you gettin' in touch with the police till you know they're safe. But to be doubly sure, Bridget will tie you up in here before we take off.' The Commander spluttered, 'You'll never make it across the Channel in this storm – it's suicide.' The wind was blowingly strongly now and white breakers were crashing on the shore. 'Well – if it's suicide, my boyo, it's you who'll be committin' it. I know you were a Navy man – well now's your chance to prove how good you were at it.' He turned to Jimmy. 'Get Bridget in here from the truck.' Jimmy looked at his father, who nodded, helpless.

The Waiting Room at Flockton Station was a calm oasis among the winds that buffeted outside. Jessica had a large earthenware pot in front of her on the centre table and was arranging a collection of ivy, wood violets, speedwell, early gorse, kingcups, anemones, celandines and coltsfoot into a delicate array of beauty. Kathy had a pile of books and papers which she was sifting through working out her final notes for the coming exam. Clancy had just woken up from an after-lunch nap, and was practising his range of whistles. 'Clancy, that goes right through my head.' Jessica sternly dropped the cover over the cage. Clancy subsided and started muttering awful dockside imprecations under his breath.

Kathy pulled her specs off and looked at the clock. 'Somebody should have been back by now. I don't like to think of your kith and kin being out in this.' Jessica was unmoved. 'Just get my kith and kin something to eat when they come in – that's all they think about.'

'What would they think of Hungarian hot-pot? Rice, sardines, baked beans, green pepper, cucumber, with just a touch of chilli?'

'It should keep them on the move at any rate.'

'Right,' Kathy said, pushing her work to one side, 'I'll set about it,' and she wandered happily into the Ticket Office.

Bob and Bill squatted on the floor of the hut, well and truly trussed, like two chickens ready for the oven. Big Hughie grinned down at them. 'That should keep you out of action. You, boy – help Bridget bring Ewan down to the boat. And you, girl, stick close by me; any idea to run away you'll hear the gaffer scream. Come on!' He frog-marched poor Commander Frost to the door and waited for the others to precede him outside. For a moment, while Big Hughie's eyes were on Jan and Bridget, Jimmy was unnoticed. He caught Bob's attention and did a swift mime. His hands went in a straight line, and then a wavy one. Then he shook his head negatively, and drew one hand in a circular motion. As Bob wondered, Big Hughie turned back and growled, 'Come on, lad!' and Jimmy had to go before him out of the door.

'How tight are your ropes, Bill?'

'I'm stuck like a 'og on a spit.'

Bob struggled to his knees. 'Can you get to your feet, though?' Bill wriggled and managed to hump himself up against the wall. 'Good man. Now listen. We've got to get in contact with *some*body. What I suggest is – if you can hop as far as the Flyer and get up in the cab – yank on the whistle lanyard with your teeth to attract attention, and keep yanking till the steam runs out. I'm going to start hopping along the line to Stogumber and try and get on the phone from there. Whichever of us strikes lucky first can alert whoever they contact about the other.'

'I dunno what it is about your family – you always seem to get in the sticky end of the water,' Bill grumbled. Bob smiled and said, 'Do your best then,' and started to hop, two legged, out of the door. As he struggled up on to the track, he heard Bill groaning behind him. Bob lolloped on like a stricken rabbit, puzzling out Jimmy's last message as he went.

Commander Frost massaged his arms and throat in the bows of the *Helen*. Behind him, Big Hughie hauled the hapless, moaning Ewan over the bulwarks and laid him in the cabin as Jimmy and Jan scrambled aboard from the dinghy, followed by Bridget. Big Hughie bent down and started the engine, which roared into life at once. The boat plunged forward, heaving at her double anchors, and Hughie thrust her into lowest gear. Then he leaped forward and hauled the bow anchor in, while Jan and Jimmy pulled in the storm anchor. Fortunately they both came free at once, and Commander Frost staggered aft to grab the tiller just in time to guide the boat away from the rocks, out of the inlet, and into the open bay. The full blast of the storm hit them as they left the shelter of the cove.

Jimmy pretended to fall with the surge of the boat and crouched alongside the gallant Commander. Black clouds were flying past the masthead as Jimmy shielded his face against the bursts of spray and rain. He saw Big Hughie looming beside Bridget in the bows, and Jan crouched beside Ewan in the cabin, and he gabbled quickly, 'I don't know if Dad understood my sign language, but I suspect that overgrown maniac probably wouldn't notice whether he was going straight or in a circle. If we take them out far enough and then turn back without them knowing, we could land again by the lighthouse on Foreland Point. Could you navigate that?'

Commander Frost gasped, 'Brilliant, sailor! Do what I can!' At that moment the engine coughed and died. Big Hughie sprang back to investigate and after a quick once over, while the boat lost way and wallowed among fleeting breakers, he bellowed, 'The petrol tank's empty. Come on, you kids – help me to raise the sails – you'll drown if you don't!'

Bob, exhausted, forced himself to plunge the last few feet along the platform at Stogumber and fell into the tiny office that housed the telephone. On the way he had finally decoded Jimmy's cryptic message – or hoped he had. A circle over waves. They would run the *Helen* in a circle – so if they went west they'd arrive at Lynton – and if east to the Burnham-on-Sea lighthouse. He managed to get the phone off the hook, praying that someone along the line would be there to answer.

Back down the track, Bill Jelly leaned on the side of the Flyer's cab and pulled once more on the whistle lanyard with his teeth. The steam was dying, but he'd had a good go for fifteen minutes and wasn't able to understand why no one had answered the wail for help. He let go the lanyard and looked down. A purple, furious face had appeared by his feet, glowering up into the cab. Percy Gwillim. 'What the *hell* are you playing at? Damnation – I'll bring this up at the public inquiry tonight – keeping that wretched thing howling all afternoon.' Bill said, 'Shut yer cake'ole and get me out of these ropes! Then I'll tell yer 'ow you can 'elp for a change – instead of 'inder!' Percy Gwillim's mouth fell open and as he untied Bill he got the whole story.

Jessica answered the telephone in the cosy twilight of the Waiting Room. She started to speak, but as her father cut her off she listened carefully. When he had finished she put the receiver down and called to Kathy, hidden by steam in the Ticket Office, 'I'm going out to phone!', grabbed her anorak and dashed out. The telephone wasn't connected to the Post Office main line and the nearest phone box was up the station approach. Jessica realized she had no money with her – then thought, 'If this isn't a 999 call I don't know what is. . . .'

The *Helen* heeled wildly as a big wave struck her. Big Hughie bawled in the Commander's ear, 'Get us ashore, you flamin' idiot – I don't care where – so long as it's somewhere in Wales!' Everyone aboard was drenched to the skin by now, except for poor Ewan, who was shielded in the cabin, and who had fainted anyway from the pain his leg had given him in the tossing boat. The Commander pointed ahead to a light that winked from the shore, 'We'll land there! Let out the mainsheet and haul on the foresail!' The wind was shrieking steady from the north. 'Thank goodness,' thought Jack Frost, 'with any luck we should have made a port tack right round to Lynton.' Jimmy and Jan hauled and let go as commanded, while Bridget occupied herself being sick over the side.

Bob, Bill and Percy Gwillim sat in the back of a police car drinking hot coffee from a thermos as they watched a spotlight play across the thundering shore at Lynton. Suddenly the beam of light caught a foundering *Helen* charging inshore sluggish but still sound, towards the tide line. There was a rending crash as the boat hit the shore and furrowed into the sand – the mainmast cracking and disintegrating under the strain. Police ran down and scrambled aboard in the streaming, gale-torn dusk.

In the Ticket Office, Kathy and Jessica heaped plates full of Hungarian hot-pot and put them on the hatch shelf for Jan to take to the table. It was nearly ten o'clock and the gale still howled outside, but the Waiting Room pulsed with warmth and conversation. It had been difficult fitting in all the family, plus Bill, Commander Frost, Basil, Geoff, and, wonder of wonders, a smiling Percy Gwillim, but somehow room had been made.

The public inquiry in the town hall had been held, and disbanded after a very short time. Mr Gwillim had been so impressed by the capture of the tearaways that he had withdrawn his opposition to FLERPS. Now he was listening like an excited schoolboy to the various yarns of the day's adventure.

Big Hughie, the chief offender, had been lugged off to jail to await trial, and poor Ewan was in hospital. Bridget was having to spend a night in jail too – but everyone hoped she would be leniently dealt with, as they thought she had been led astray and was not actually criminal. And, best of all, there was no single hero; everyone had played their parts, even, as a somewhat stiff Commander Frost remarked after his first mouthful of hot-pot, Kathy and Jessica. For anyone who could produce such 'an extraordinarily famous repast' deserved mention in dispatches just as much as those who had taken a more physical part in the actions of that exciting day.

CHAPTER 6
CIRCUS SIDE-SHOW

Spring, so far, had been very wet indeed, with flooding in Flockton and Watchet; then, halfway through April, came a lovely sky-washed day of sun and wind. Jessica put a last placard outside Clancy's corner of her makeshift zoo. With Jimmy's help she had partitioned off an area, including the old, disused coal bunker where the animals were kept, and given each one a separate corner, with their own personal notice fastened to the fence. Underneath the name of each creature was the Latin name of its breed – the same as in a real zoo.

Trivet's shed and small paddock filled one corner (*Equus non vulgaris* – uncommon horse); then there was Dick Duck (*anas peculiaris* – unusual duck) in his wired off pool; Piglet, a reward for services rendered from a kindly disposed neighbouring farmer, rooted in the mud. His card read *Porcus roseacus* (pink pig). Nuisance the cat (*Feles naturalis* – domestic cat) was temporarily enclosed in a wired-in run, and not liking it very much; of course, she would only be in there when the zoo was open – just for an hour or two – then she'd be out again, prowling around. Clancy the cockatoo (*Psittacus arboris* – tree parrot) sidled up and down his perch next door muttering, 'That it should come to this . . .' and rolling his eyes like a bad actor. Pest bleated from her pen for more hay, then tried to nibble her own card (*Caper montis* – mountain goat), but it was thoughtfully fixed just out of her reach. Jessica checked the hens (*Gallinae rarae* – rare hens), and looked round approvingly at the big notice by the entrance, which read FLOCKTON STATION ZOO – ADMISSION 5p; pretty good value, Jessica thought.

She heard squelching feet crossing the muddy yard and turned to find Percy Gwillim looking round the zoo with reluctant admiration. Since the public inquiry he had been very pleasant, and had even come round to accepting the idea of the FLERPS reopening for scheduled services in June. In fact he now seemed a little envious of the Carter family and their slightly crazy way of life; Jessica couldn't help feeling a bit sorry for the lonely old crust.

The crust muttered, 'Good – good. Yes – yes . . . excellent value for five p . . . Like the Latin touch – very realistic – hrrrmph!' Jessica thanked him for the compliment and asked him if she could help him at all. He frumped and fribbled incomprehensibly for a few moments and then asked Jessica if her zoo could be on the itinerary of the children's outing which he had organized as Chairman of the Flockton Round Table. This was a group of men got together to help people who couldn't help themselves. They were inviting all the school-children of Flockton, aged eleven and under, to the circus, up the line at Bishop's Lydeard. It was to take place the next Saturday and the Flyer was going to take them there. Percy thought it would be a good idea if they could look round Jessica's zoo before they left, '. . . sort of get them in the mood . . .', he explained.

Jessica was thrilled – her first paying public. She needed the money badly to pay for more fencing, for neither she nor Jan nor Jimmy had had any spending money for weeks; things were a bit pinched in the Carter family. Percy Gwillim grunted acknowledgement and splashed back across the yard towards his Land-Rover. Jessica looked round again at her zoological collection. If only some of them could do something – like in a circus. What an attraction that would be! Then an idea slid into her head, and she pondered a moment, looking carefully again at each one in turn.

Faintly, from the far side of the station buildings, came the the sound of a voice speaking a foreign language through a loud-speaker. Jan watched from the signal box as a small party of Bavarian railway enthusiasts got back on their chartered charabanc to go to Dartmouth for an excursion up the Dart Valley. Jan smelt the fresh salt breeze sweeping up from Blue Anchor

Bay and decided she wasn't cut out to be a ticket-seller or a guide – even though, on this occasion, her school German had come in quite useful. Then she saw a young boy coming round the corner from the engine sheds. He looked a little older than herself, very slim, with tousled bronze curls, grey eyes and a lazy smile. He had a small scar on his chin that Jan found quite attractive. He came hesitantly over to her.

'*Sprechen Sie Deutsch?*' Jan nodded and said, '*Jawohl.*' The boy relaxed at once and said, '*Kannst du mir bitte sagen ob der Bus nach Taunton schon abgefahren ist?*' Jan translated to herself that the lad wanted to know if the Taunton bus had gone. He must have got it wrong – the other Germans had just left in the opposite direction. No, he explained, he was not with that party; he wanted to get back to the circus at Bishop's Lydeard. He wasn't sure where the bus went from. Jan said, '*Komm bitte mit mir.*' The boy smiled gratefully at being understood and followed her to the station gate where Jan pointed out the bus shelter down the road. The boy took her hand and shook it politely, saying: '*Das ist sehr freundlich von dir,*' then smiled and went off down the road. Like a free tiger, or leopard, Jan thought, and wondered if he actually worked in the circus. If he did, then she envied him. She wished she could go to the circus herself, but she knew there wasn't one penny left in her mother's jam-jar even for necessities – let alone for amusement. Jan looked sadly down the length of Platform Two. She could see her mother talking urgently to her father as he made some adjustment by the rear wheels of the Flyer. The sweet old engine hissed an old railway song to herself as she took her ease in the siding.

Bob and Kathy were both equally worried, and equally at a loss. It was a very simple problem that they knew a lot of people had to face – but that didn't make it any easier. There was no cash left in the kitty. They lived quite frugally, but the wages Bob got from FLERPS just were not going as far as they once had. Kathy was wondering if Commander Frost could make Bob an advance – just to pay the bill at Mr Fosdyke's. He was their grocer, and a very friendly man. But Kathy had begun to feel guilty every time she went in there now, to buy food that would be 'put down' in their red account book.

Bob was reluctant to ask for more money as he knew the Society wasn't too keen to pay out and was worried the Commander might offer him something from his own pocket, which would be very embarrassing. Kathy asked, 'Do you think we could make a charge for Percy Gwillim's outing?' Bob shook his head. 'The money would have to go to the Society – and anyway it's supposed to be free. Percy's Round Table will be paying expenses, of course – but none of that will come our way.' Kathy looked glum. She would have gone out to work herself, but she hadn't long to go before her final degree exams and she did so want to pass. She hated troubling Bob, but something had to be done.

He turned from tightening a nut on the crosshead. 'I'm taking the old girl up to Bishop's Lydeard this afternoon to pump out that flood water from the old engine shed there. I'll have a word with Jack Frost – see if he has any suggestions. There's nothing else I can do, is there?' Kathy agreed. All three children badly needed new school shoes before the summer term started the following week. Bob gave Kathy a kiss, which, as usual, tasted slightly of oil, and she wandered back to the Waiting Room to try to improvise a cheap nourishing stew for their evening meal.

Jimmy and Jan walked along the track towards Bill Jelly's hut. On either side of them the sun and wind chased along the high hills above the sea, drying out some of the previous day's downpour. Both of them knew of the family financial crisis, for there were few secrets among them, and problems that affected them all were always discussed openly.

Jimmy had suggested to Jan that Bill might have some ideas for raising cash. He'd been everywhere and done everything. 'Like robbing a bank?' Jan asked. Jimmy grinned. 'You never know – and there's always a first time.' Jan was serious. 'If only there was some way we could help – I feel so useless – just a sort of hanger-on.' Jimmy heaved at a small branch that had blown down to the line and flung it well clear. 'If we did paper rounds and things we wouldn't be able to help Dad and Mum at the station – and we're all needed to get the line into working order again – one way or t'other. Next year when we've passed our exams and the service is running we'll be off their hands. Then I can go on my computer course, and, with your foreign languages, you could go anywhere in the world practically.' Jan thought of the circus at Bishop's

Lydeard and how much she would like to join them. And, maybe the German boy.

As they turned a bend in the track Bill's hut showed ahead. They both noticed that, for the first time, there was no smoke coming from the chimney. All at once they wondered if something was wrong, and started to run towards the hut; then they stopped, as suddenly the door opened and a strange figure confronted them. Bill Jelly as was – but what a difference. He had shaved, for a start, and combed his hair, which now curled in distinguished silver ringlets over the collar of a pin-stripe jacket that had been home-cleaned and home-pressed to match the well-creased trousers beneath. Old leather shoes were on his feet, which, though cracked, gleamed in the sun, and a neat tie was knotted under the collar of a worn but clean shirt. Bill now looked like a slightly eccentric millionaire antique collector.

He seemed a bit thrown at meeting Jan and Jimmy, but tried to pass it off nonchalantly. 'Turned out nice again, ent it? Just fancied a stroll over to the town. Got to keep in trim entcher?' Jimmy and Jan looked disbelieving, mouths half open, as Bill stepped daintily over the little footbridge, across the ditch that separated the hut from the track. Jimmy nudged Jan. 'We'll take a stroll with you if that's all right?' Bill looked at a loss, then showed his yellow teeth in a forced smile. 'Please yourselves.' He started up the track towards Bishop's Lydeard, past wind-dried bays of hawthorn and blossoming May. As they walked, Jan and Jimmy talked about the family's financial problems and Bill looked concerned.

Finally he stopped and said, 'All right – I'll come clean.' Jimmy quipped, 'You couldn't possibly come cleaner than you are!' and, as Bill looked put out, Jan inserted the usual hasty apology, 'Jim's jokes.' Bill blinked and said, 'I ent goin' to be around much longer.' Jimmy said, 'You mean they finally caught up with you?', but Jan ssshed him and asked worriedly, 'Is your complaint getting worse?' Bill was impatient. 'No. I mean I'm leavin.' Time to move on. I bin 'ere long enough. I'm goin' for a interview.'

Jimmy looked at Bill's neatly pressed suit and asked, 'Going into the banking business, are you?' Bill was irritated. 'If you're goin' to keep sendin' me up I shan't tell you,' and walked on. The two youngsters caught him up, Jimmy apologizing, and, as they walked, Bill told them he had been getting restless lately and had decided to apply for a job in the circus. Jan was excited, but Jimmy said, 'Why dress up like that?' Bill explained that he'd stand more chance if he looked 'respekable and trussworthy'. Circuses wouldn't take on just any old layabout.

The two youngsters were quiet, sadly contemplating life without Bill Jelly. In the windy silence they heard a well-known howl behind them. The Flyer was rounding Crowcombe bend and coming up fast. They stood at the side of the track and signalled. Bob braked alongside, looking pleased but slightly bewildered. He too was rather taken aback at Bill's appearance. Bob had been going to ask him to help pump out the engine sheds, but didn't like to now. Jimmy would do instead, however, and he joined his father on the footplate while Jan and Bill joined Jessie in the truck behind.

They were astonished to find Pest in there with her, but as the Flyer moved off, Jessica explained that she was taking the goat to the circus to pick up a few tips on how to get animals to perform interesting acts of their own free will. Bill joked that Pest never did anything that wasn't of her own free will – but Jan disapproved strongly of animals being taught undignified tricks. Bill defended Jessica. 'So long as they're not forced to . . .' he said as the Flyer rumbled and clanked through Combe Florey halt, '. . . they enjoys it . . .' He noticed Pest chewing his shoe-lace, '. . . and I'm quite sure your little perisher will just fancy showin' herself off in public.'

The great ten-acre field on the outskirts of Bishop's Lydeard looked like a harbour for ancient galleons as the tents and flags billowed and flapped in the wind and bunting flourished in the sun. Many people were about, busying themselves with preparations. The Big Top was up, but there were all sorts of jobs to be done before that evening's performance – test the equipment, prepare the hot dogs and hamburgers, candy floss and lemonade, get the side-shows ready, feed the animals, clear away rubbish and still leave time for the circus folk to have their own snack.

Bill Jelly wandered among the ropes and pegs and caravans looking for Mr Sylvester – the owner and manager of the whole colourful kaleidoscope. Some people told Bill one way, and some another, most of them friendly enough. There was a covered rank for the elephants and another two for the circus ponies and horses. There were cages for the lions, tigers and two panthers, and cages for gorillas and a very unhappy rhinoceros. Stacked on a long loader were hundreds of bales of hay, bought that day from a local farmer, and beside these stood a short, plump, pink, perspiring, pop-eyed gentleman in a scarlet jersey, breeches and top boots. Mr Sylvester himself. Bill Jelly straightened his unaccustomed tie, pulled at his jacket, and, summoning up his courage, approached the barking firework.

Jan had wandered off on her own, feeling very sour and empty. She didn't care for animals in cages and had spoken very sharply to Jessica, who had then gone her own way. Bill hadn't wanted company in his quest for employment, and Jimmy and her father had told her there was no help she could give at the pumps in Bishop's Lydeard Station. The sun was lying lower now, and as Jan passed some bushes on the fringe of the encampment a flash of brilliance caught her eye.

She looked round the bushes and there before her was the German boy she had met that morning, dressed in a golden suit of spangles and doing amazing hand-stands across the green turf. 'He must be one of the acrobatic team,' Jan thought, and then he saw her, stopped, breathless, and smiled. Jan's heart stood still. He was very beautiful. He came over. Jan organized her brain to greet him in his own language.

Jan said, '*Es freut mich Sie wiederzusehen,*' then immediately felt stricken with shyness. The boy seemed to understand, for he took up a woollen robe from the hedge, wrapped it about him like a cloak, and invited Jan to look round the circus with him. Jan's heart filled with delight. He took her hand gently in his and led her towards the wild-animal cages. Jan felt the blood in her cheeks as she said, '*Ich heisse Janet. Was ist dein Name?*' The youth beamed and replied, '*Gerhard Steiffel.*' As Janet felt his gaze on her, she became deeply conscious of her rumpled wind-tossed hair and her rather muddy duffel coat. How she wished she was more presentable.

Down at Bishop's Lydeard Station, Bob and Jimmy watched the brown flood water gurgle out of the end of the pipe that wound back into the engine shed. The improvised pump was operating off the steam power from the Flyer, through a device of Bob's contriving, and the shed was nearly dry now. A familiar figure stalked along the track towards them and bellowed, 'Clearin' the bilges? First rate! Man the pumps and all hands on deck – can I help? Oh.' At that moment the pump gave an awful coughing gasp and the last trickle of water oozed from the end of the canvas pipe. Jack Frost breezed on, 'Always the same – I arrive to help just as the dirty work finishes. Think we'll get this little anchorage ship-shape soon?'

He looked round the weed-covered flags of the Up Platform of Bishop's Lydeard Station. Bob grunted as he began to coil the pipe with Jimmy's help, 'Depends on what assistance we get from the other members. Funny how most FLERPS members always manage to turn out for pleasure jaunts – but when there's work to be done – less than ten per cent are available.' The Commander winked heavily. 'Ah – but they ain't paid for it like you are – ey?'

Bob winced. How was he to broach the subject of their being so broke? And without embarrassing the Commander? Jimmy saved Bob the trouble. 'D'you realize you've got five labourers on one wage?' Frost's eyes crinkled questioningly, 'Eh? What?' Jimmy pursued the subject defiantly. 'It's not your fault, I know – but the Board's got one fully paid driver and four part-time slaves. Mum, Jan, Jess and me – we help all the time, don't we – on and off? What's the Board going to do about it? If things carry on the way they are they'll have a strike on their hands and then where'll the Grand Opening be?' Bob smiled to himself. Nothing like coming straight out with it – just the way he'd always hoped his children would be.

Commander Frost was flustered, 'Yers . . . well . . . dodgy cross currents there. Board's close to the wind as it is – don't want a capsize. However – ha'pporths of tar and all that. Harrah! Harrrumph! Hah!! Have to see what we can do. Four more wage packets. Hell's teeth! They won't buy that.' Jimmy retorted, 'Five more with Bill Jelly – why should he be left out? And if they don't buy it they can lump it.' That sounded a bit odd, but the Commander knew what was meant. He went pink and stuttered, 'Yes yes – s-sorry – s-sink me in gin – have to see Frisby – see what can do – shame . . . I'll cut adrift then – let you know.' He moved away to

his car, looking very upset. Jimmy glanced at his father. 'Am I right or am I wrong?' Bob grinned. 'You're right, son,' and Jimmy grinned back. 'So *that*'s all right! Let's get this pipe back on board.' They set to, coiling it towards the Flyer.

Jessica was trailing Pest round the outside of the field, looking for someone who wasn't too busy. She had asked one Spanish-looking lady in dungarees if she knew how to train goats, and the lady had waved her hands and sworn at her in, presumably, Spanish. Then Jessica had shown Pest to a large Cockney practising eating fire near a brazier. He had been kind but coughy. He had wheezed the information that the person Jessica should see was the lady who ran the performing poodle act – Serena Salubria. At last Jessica found her, but only after Pest had butted one irate attendant and pinched a row of flags from the fortune-teller's tent. Jessica had hastily stuffed them back in the flap and pressed on to where she could see a group of black-and-white poodles squatting round a caravan. Pest gave a great jerk and pulled her halter from Jessica's grasp.

The poodles shrieked and charged, all together, knocking Jessica flat in their eagerness to pulverize Pest. Then a large lady screamed from the caravan and the poodles retreated back under the wheels, leaving Jessica dazed and Pest running round and round a guy-rope that her halter had caught on.

Jessica was fighting tears as she scrambled to her feet. Serena Salubria was shouting from the steps of her caravan, 'Get away from here – you silly insufficient child! And take that pest with with you!' As Jessica turned to the goat, a gruff voice said, 'Cheer up – at least she got 'er name right.'

It was Bill Jelly, looking a bit downcast himself. In a moment he had untwisted Pest, caught hold of Jessica's hand and led them both out of Madame Salubria's earshot. Jessica blurted out her tale of woe – how no one seemed to have time or inclination to help her train Pest. Bill muttered sympathy and then confided his own tale of woe. Mr Sylvester had no job for him. No work at all. Bill sniffed. 'So it looks as though I'm landed with you lot, after all – for a time yet, anyway.' Jessica smiled. 'I hope we're not as bad as all that.' Then she looked woebegone again. 'Oh, Bill! If only the animals were more *use*! I wouldn't feel so bad about us having to buy stuff to feed them when we're so broke.'

Bill comforted her. ''Ens give you eggs, don't they? Clancy's a sort of watch-dog in a way, Nuisance keeps the mice down, Trivet gives you dung for the vegetables, and given time Dick Duck and Piglet – ' He stopped himself just in time. He'd been about to say 'a few square meals', but he coughed and went on hastily, 'Nothin' like goats. Pest gives yer milk, don't she?' Jessica nodded. 'Nearly a gallon a day at the moment.' 'There y'are, then. An' I'll tell you another thing. Goats are marvellous with 'orses. Always keep a goat in stables – anything goes wrong they calm the 'orses. 'Orses trust a goat, d'y'see?' They were strolling towards the edge of the field now, where the railway track ran down to the town. Bill saw a hot-dog stall and asked Jessica, 'Fancy one? My treat?' Jessica smiled broadly and said: 'Thank you, Bill.' Then she added, 'For everything.'

Unknown to Jessica and Bill, just behind the hot-dog stall Gerhard was showing Jan the two black panthers rippling up and down in their cage, discontented. Jan hated free creatures in cages, but at the moment she was more aware of the fact that as she stared at the panthers, Gerhard was staring at her. Jan had found herself speaking quite fluently in her school German, and had been telling Gerhard about working on the railway and how they hoped to open it to the public soon. Gerhard asked, '*Müssen die Leute bezahlen wenn sie die Eisenbahn benutzen?*' He wanted to know if people bought tickets to travel on their railway. Jan nodded as she tried to translate into German, but his next sentence drove all thought from her head.

'. . . *aber . . . du bist wirklich sehr nett . . .*' – 'but . . . you seem so graceful . . .' Jan blushed and with her throat like iron pipe whispered, '*Ich kann leider nicht verstehen wie ich es machen muss,*' telling him she didn't know quite what he meant. Then he said: '*Tanzt du gerne?*' – 'Do you like dancing?' Now could it possibly be that this golden youth was offering to take her out? Jan could scarcely breathe with excitement. Then, just as Gerhard seemed about to make his invitation, he stopped and sniffed. Then he spoke urgently, '*Komm schon!*' – and leaped round the back of the cage. Jan followed, and saw Gerhard stepping swiftly towards

77

the trailer of hay that was parked there. One corner of it was flaring fiercely where some bales had been removed for feeding and loose hay had been strewn about. It was impossible to tell what had started it, but there was no time for wondering about that now, as the flames, fanned by the wind, were consuming the hay greedily.

Gerhard yelled, '*Achtung!*' and looked around desperately for assistance. Then he called for Jan to help him. She wrenched off her duffel coat as Gerhard grabbed a bit of sacking and they both beat at the flames – but it was of little use. As the fire roared up the side of the stack two circus men came into the space, looked, yelled and ran for buckets. Bits of hay, blown by the wind, were alighting on nearby tents and the panthers screeched, panicking as they smelt the smoke.

One of the men shouted, 'I'll call the Fire Brigade!' and ran off. Jan grabbed Gerhard's arm. Over the yells and the crackling flames she shouted at him to come with her to the station. She couldn't think of the German word for pump, but Gerhard realized she knew what she was at when she screamed out the word for 'train'. Together they ran to the edge of the field and turned down the railway track towards the town. Gerhard in his light shoes was soon far ahead of her, but Jan, breathless, pounded on.

Bill and Jessica heard the sounds of alarm and went to see what was up, munching their hot dogs as they went. They gasped as they saw a bundle of flaring hay catch on the canvas of the horse lines; terrified neighs came from inside. Jessica threw the remains of her hot dog away, and grabbed Pest back from Bill. 'Now's the chance to prove yourself, goatling!' she cried, and darted away, Pest cavorting alongside. Bill called, 'Hey! Watch yourself!' and then shambled after her, protesting caution.

Inside the horse lines three men were cursing and swearing as the horses stood, nostrils wide, eyes staring, quivering in fear but hooves rooted to the earth. The head horseman bellowed, 'They won't move – they're too frightened!' The side of the canvas had caught now and the wind was tearing a great orange gash of fire across it. Jessica was frightened. She knew that if the horses did panic there wouldn't be much left of her under those hooves – but she gulped down her fear and led Pest under the nose of the first horse – a big black gelding. With her free hand she untied its

halter rope, and pulled Pest so that the little goat put her hooves
up on her waist and nuzzled the black giant above her.

Jessica clicked comfortingly, and pulled gently on the halter.
Amazingly the great horse followed Pest past the widening burn-
ing gash. As they came out, Bill was there, sweating and helping
other eager hands to take the horse from Jessica and lead it away.
She called to Bill, 'Come *on*! Let's try the others!' and ducked
back in with Pest. Bill followed, groaning but determined.

A wild toot floated on the wind as the Flyer panted up the track
to the edge of the field. Bob, Gerhard, Jimmy and Jan quickly
uncoiled the hose-pipe. Jimmy took one end and threw it in the
an old pit full of water that lay in one corner of the field, while
Jan and Gerhard carried the other end across to the long loader.
Bob checked the junction, then leaped up on the footplate and
pulled over the regulator. Power coursed through the Flyer,
diverted by Bob's ingenuity, from the driving pistons to his
makeshift pump.

Thump – thump – thump – a jet of water shot between Jan and
Gerhard, hanging on to the end of the jerking pipe, and hissed
over the blazing pyramid of hay. In the distance the nasal klaxon
of a fire engine could be heard as it bounced across the field in
support. The crew had certainly got there in record time – but had
it not been for the Flyer the fire might well have got beyond their
control.

The sky was dark as the flames died, and a hundred faces
gleamed white and grim in the coloured circus lights. Mr Sylvester
squelched across to the Flyer, where Commander Frost, a little
late as usual, was heartily congratulating Bob and Jimmy on their
swift rescue operation. Behind Mr Sylvester came Jessica, Pest
and Bill. The circus owner was hoarse in his praise and thanks,
but Bob gently cut him short, and told him they were glad they'd
been able to help. He was anxious to get his soaked family home
to dry out, for not all the water had gone on the fire. They all
piled on the truck, and with a farewell toot the Flyer started home,
sent on her way by a cheer from the assembled circus folk. Mr
Sylvester caught hold of the Commander's arm and began talking
to him urgently.

Jan felt chilled from the skin in. She had not joined the Flyer
and in the mêlée no one had missed her. She was anxious to see
Gerhard again, but he had disappeared in the shadows of the tents

and caravans. Jan trudged between the pools of light, looking this
way and that for her golden German acrobat.

She was missed in the Waiting Room at Flockton Station where
Bob, Jimmy, Bill and Jessica were gulping hot soup by a roaring
fire. Kathy had been assured by Jimmy and Bob that they had
both seen Jan in good fettle after the fire, and as it was still only
half past six, they weren't too worried; Bob said he'd go back and
look for Janet if she wasn't home in fifteen minutes. There was a
bang on the door at that point and Commander Frost blew in.

He was looking very sheepish. 'About that . . . er . . . business.
I rang Frisby and he said there's nothing the Board can do.' Bob
glanced at Kathy and shrugged. She made a face, but her eyes
were loving. 'We'll manage somehow,' she said. Both of them
heard only the end of the Commander's next sentence, '. . . two
hundred pounds.' Jimmy was looking delighted and Clancy from
his corner screeched 'Pieces of eight!' He had always been a bit of
a ham. The Commander explained again to Bob and Kathy. Mr
Sylvester, the circus owner, was going to make a claim on his
insurance, but in the meantime he had pressed on the Commander
nearly two hundred pounds in cash, the whole of the previous
night's takings. 'Saved by the bell – eh? – Or should I say – by the
whistle?' 'Right,' Bob said. 'That's marvellous – put it in the jam-
jar, Kathy. I'm going to search for Jan.'

Jan was sitting in Gerhard's caravan sipping from a mug of hot
coffee. Gerhard's mother and father were still outside doing their
share in clearing up the mess. Gerhard was speaking quietly. He
explained that the circus was moving on the next day. He was
sorry he would not see Jan again. He liked dancing too. Perhaps
they might meet one day. There was a lump in Janet's throat as
she got up to go. '*Das verstehe ich sehr gut*' – but it wasn't true –
she didn't understand. She didn't understand why you could, in
one short day, be filled with so much delight and excitement, and
in the same day lose it all.

As Gerhard's father and mother came up the caravan steps,
smiling in friendship, Jan pulled her damp scorched duffel coat
closer about her and ran, tearfully, into the ring of dark outside

81

the lights. Her father said nothing when he met her on the road home – for he was understanding too, and knew that only time might help her.

Which, of course, it did.

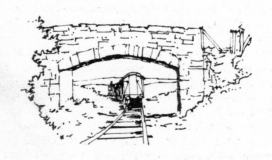

CHAPTER 7
POP GOES THE FLYER!

'D-Day minus ten – and what have we got to show for it?' asked Jimmy. Jessica blinked. 'I wish you wouldn't use these funny expressions – you only have to explain them afterwards and it wastes so much time.' They were sitting on the edge of Platform One, watching flies buzz around a blob of jam that had dropped on the track from a sandwich Jessica was munching. Jimmy sighed. 'You've heard Dad talk about it – in the war when he was a schoolboy at Folkestone he saw the troops going across to France on D-Day.' 'What's that got to do with anything?' Jessica had on one of her most annoyingly superior expressions. Jimmy cunningly caught the crust that she threw to one side and munched it morosely.

'Ten days to the Grand Opening . . . the biggest day of our lives – and no flags, no brass band organized, no ceremony – certainly the biggest day in Dad's life – and as far as I can see it's just going to fizzle away into nothing.' Jessica pointed down the platform. 'There are posters advertising it and Bill was saying he'd heard the people talking about it in the Exciseman.' Jimmy looked exasperated. 'But you've got to *sell* something like this – attract people; all Dad's concerned with is how well the engine goes.' 'That is quite important, after all,' Jessica replied, 'and it does take up most of his time – perhaps we should try to organize some other attractions. There's my zoo – people would be interested to see that.'

Jan joined them on the edge of the platform. 'You two plotting something – or shouldn't I know?'

'We want to try and make something grand out of the Grand Opening. All Jessica's come up with is her zoo. A horse, a goat and a cat!'

Jessica looked upset. 'And the hens and Dick Duck and Piglet – not to mention Clancy.'

Jan agreed, 'Don't let's mention Clancy – he's moulting. Anyway, they're only domestic animals – people have seen them all before.'

Jessica was cross. 'Not our versions of them – they're very individual!' She looked accusingly at her brother and sister. 'What ideas have you two got, anyway?' 'Well,' Jimmy answered, 'a brass band for a start – and they should play our signature tune!'

Jan looked blank. 'What signature tune?' To which Jimmy replied, 'The one I'm writing with Tink Filmer.'

Jimmy had had this vision for some weeks. A hit tune played on the local radio to advertise the Flyer; and he and Tink had been working on it in the lunch break at school. Tink was a natural musician and could play the guitar and piano and the harmonica. He had already sketched out a melody to match the words Jimmy had written – all they needed now was a group or a band to back it.

There was a happy hoot from up the line and the green-and-gold Flyer puffed round the bend. The children scrambled to their feet on the edge of the platform as the engine clanked to a halt in front of them. Bob Carter shut off steam and leaped down to join them; Commander Frost followed him more gingerly. As they all strolled across to the Waiting Room, Jimmy said, 'Dad – we were thinking – we've got to do something about the Grand Opening. Otherwise it'll be the biggest damp squib since Guy Fawkes.' Bob grinned and said, 'I don't know what more you want. Mrs Frost is opening it in the largest hat outside Ascot and smashing a bottle of champagne across the bows.' He winked sideways at the Commander. 'The Bishop's Lydeard Silver Band are playing us off, and we've three hundred flags and bunting from the Combe Florey British Legion. What else would you like?' Jimmy looked crestfallen.

Commander Frost butted in. 'I don't suppose I could drive her a bit, could I?' Bob shook his head. It was essential to have a licence to drive locomotives and the test wasn't easy. The Commander persisted. 'Only a few yards – I've watched yer and it looks so easy. I've always wanted to drive a puffer train ever since I was tiny . . .' His eyes began to swim with thwarted ecstasy. Jan, Jimmy and Jessica looked away, hiding their smiles behind their hands. Bob was adamant. 'No way, Jack. Not even twelve inches. If anyone found out goodness knows what would happen.' Jack Frost sighed. 'Oh well – no harm in askin'. Just wanted to be part of things, that's all – not to worry.' And he wandered away to his car, looking a bit dismal.

Bob, Jan and Jessica went into the Waiting Room to clean up, but Jimmy, after an instant think, followed Commander Frost to his car. 'D'you sing?' he asked abruptly. Frost looked puzzled. 'Sing? You mean shanties and Gilbert and Sullivan and all that?' Jimmy nodded. 'Sort of.' Jack Frost's face cleared. ''S matter of fact, an operatic chappie who was well up in that sort of thing once told me I had quite a good bathroom baritone.' Jimmy looked pleased. 'Good. Meet me at Bill Jelly's hut tomorrow at five o'clock and we'll have a practice. Bill's a tenor – so that fits – and he's strumming a sort of home-made biscuit box bass and Tink Filmer's bringing his guitar and maybe we can even teach it to the band by the Opening.' Frost wasn't catching up very fast. 'Teach who what?' 'The Song of the Flyer', said Jimmy. 'Five o'clock tomorrow – right?' The Commander looked bemused, but nodded. 'Right you are, sailor.' He then started his motor and drove rather uncertainly out of the yard.

As Jimmy joined the rest of the family in the Waiting Room, Bob was unrolling a large sheet of paper and spreading it on the table. It was a detailed time schedule of the events of the Grand Opening. Kathy looked over his shoulder admiringly. 'Very impressive – you are a clever husband.' Bob rattled through the time-table. 'Steam up on the Flyer nine a.m. Jack Frost comes to cross-check arrangements ten a.m. We go down to Lane End and do a check there – back to Flockton eleven a.m. The band starts playing and the public starts arriving eleven-ten – eleven-forty Grand Opening by Althea Frost and at eleven-fifty-nine on the dot the Flyer leaves Flockton on the first scheduled public trip to Lane End. There.'

Jimmy looked dubious. 'You think it'll work? I mean, it only needs one thing to come unstuck for the whole works to be gummed up.' Kathy corrected him with 'That's a mixed metaphor.'

Jimmy grinned. 'Get the university madam – better a mixed metaphor than a mixed-up opening.' Bob was brisk. 'No need to worry – it'll all be as smooth as pie.' Kathy was about to correct him too, but he didn't give her a chance with 'Now – shall we eat? I'm starving.' And they all sat down to Kathy's summer speciality 'Rabbit's Paradise', bits of every kind of salad vegetable imaginable, plus a few unimaginable; very colourful and crunchy and, as Jimmy commented, 'Crude food!'

The next ten days seemed to whizz past in manic activity. Jessica designed new cards to put above the animals' compounds, and groomed them for longer each day until Jan protested that they wouldn't have any fur or feathers left. Bob oiled and polished the engine till it dazzled in the sun. Kathy organized refreshments and people to help and Jan biked back and forth carrying messages and countermanding instructions till she was quite saddle-sore. Jimmy disappeared each afternoon to Bill's hut where he and Bill, plus the Commander and Tink Filmer, practised their musical surprise till it had a super professional gloss. The Commander had been persuaded to rattle on a washboard with thimbled fingers as extra percussion. 'Sort of skifflish . . .?' he murmured, surprising them all. Mr Jenkins, the tiny gnome who conducted the Silver Band, had had parts copied out for his bandsmen and on the night before the Grand Opening there was a final rehearsal in the band room which went off nigh perfectly. Mr Jenkins was a devil for discipline and not given to praise – but even he admitted it was a jolly tune and should be much appreciated. As everyone dispersed after the practice, Bill Jelly refused a lift from Jack Frost and walked home down the track by himself.

The Grand Opening was giving him itchy feet. He was beginning to feel it was time he moved on. Sitting up in bed with his mug of hot sweet cocoa he regarded a tattered poster that he had found blowing down the railway line. It advertised a big agricultural show on in Taunton for a week, including a fun-fair and sideshows. Bill sipped and thought. There should be a job for him of some kind in a show like that. He looked reflectively round the battered hut and wondered vaguely if he would miss it much. Then he shrugged and gulped his cocoa. Can't stop in the same place forever. Makes you old before your time. He'd give the Grand

Opening a miss. The Carters could do without him now and Bill hated goodbyes. Just fade out – that was the best way.

The Great Day dawned, sunny and windless and hot. Everything seemed in readiness. Mr Jenkins and his band were practising their introductory music, keeping Jimmy and Tink's piece as a surprise for the moment just before the Flyer moved off. Flockton Station looked very gay and patriotic with garlands of Union Jacks and flowers and multicoloured bunting. There was a tape strung across the track in front of the Flyer, who was hissing contentedly to herself by Platform One. Next to the tape was a small dais with a bottle of champagne tied with red-and-gold ribbon and hung from a cradle suspended from the station roof. Commander Frost had checked everything with Bob and wandered off to make sure his slightly vague lady hadn't lost herself in a siding. Jessica was putting a caged Clancy in a small pen with Nuisance, who had a large yellow bow tied round her neck. Kathy was counting sandwiches in the Parcels Office – temporarily a Refreshment Room, and Jan was giving a final sweep to the platform before going to help Jessica sell tickets. One large lady in a straw hat and a dress like a flower show was already waiting by the station entrance for the gate to be opened. The first of hundreds it was to be hoped.

Bob and Jimmy stood by the band, watching Mr Jenkins gesticulating them through 'Rule Britannia' – *fortissimo*. Bob bellowed in Jimmy's ear, 'I told you there was nothing to worry about. Fifty-seven minutes to go and everything's in apple-pie order, no hitches so far!' Jimmy looked happy. 'You don't know about my surprise yet.' Bob shouted, 'What surprise?' and Jimmy carried on above the thumping of the band. 'My surprise comes when the Flyer leaves the platform – ' He turned to look at the engine and his eyes popped. Bob yelled, 'What?' Jimmy mouthed without being heard, 'My surprise is that we haven't got an engine!'

Bob's gaze followed his pointing finger. Where the Flyer had stood was the emptiest space either of them had ever seen. Leaving Mr Jenkins and the band blissfully unaware of the unthinkable, Bob and Jimmy ran over to the Parcels Office. Kathy looked up as Bob whinnied, 'Where's the – have you – who's taken our train?' Kathy giggled, 'You're having me on,' then realized he was serious. 'I did see – a couple of minutes ago – Jack Frost get up on the footplate.' Bob howled, 'Oh no! He must have been playing engine drivers – and we didn't hear a thing over the noise of the band!'

Bob rapped out, 'Kathy, you telephone ahead down to Basil at Stogumber and ask if he's seen anything go past – if not – tell him to push the points over on to the siding. Jimmy and I'll pump the maintenance truck down the line and see if we can find anything more than a heap of scrap iron! Come on!' And he and Jimmy ran out towards the hand truck on Platform Three.

Commander Frost stood upon the footplate of the Flyer as she chuffed naughtily down the track at fifteen miles an hour. How the gin-struck blazes did you stop the wretched thing? He yanked on the whistle lanyard and as it hooted he wailed in company, 'Where do we go for honey now . . .?'

Basil Humpthorn finished putting a last lick of pink paint on the lamp-post at Stogumber Halt and stepped back, well satisfied. No one would get off here on the Grand Opening trial run, but they wanted the little halts to look as bright as possible as the Flyer chuffed past . . . Basil heard a whistle up the line and in moments the Flyer was upon him. Basil caught a glimpse of a pink face and waving arms and then the telephone bell started clanging and he dived into the office.

Bill Jelly mooched moodily along the track towards Lane End. He was strung about with cases and carrier bags and string bags and parcels – no matter how often he told himself to travel light he always ended up looking like a left-luggage counter. Bill came to a division in the line. The main track led on to Lane End; the side track led two hundred yards to a set of buffers backed by a disused sand-pit. The sun was hot and Bill was thirsty. He thought to himself, 'Two miles and I can stop off at the Headless Horseman for a large pint of hop-juice.' Then he felt the track tremble beneath him and simultaneously heard a hoot from behind. Looking back up the track, he saw the Flyer bearing down on him. Leaning far out from the footplate was the torso of the Commander, waving a red flag and yelling, 'Fore! Clear the way! Help!' Bill acted with surprising agility. Scattering bags and parcels on all sides, he leaped to the set points at the junction. Geoff Gosling had been down the line oiling all the points a month ago, but had unaccountably missed this one.

As the Flyer neared the junction Bill heaved at the handle – nothing but squeaks and grinding groans. Bill heaved again, sweat breaking out on his forehead. Then, just as the Flyer reached the dividing rail, there was a clang and the points swung across. Bill yelled something up at the Commander as he thumped past, but all the old sailor could make out was '. . . anti-clockwise . . .' He looked at the levers and wheels in front of him. 'Hell's teeth! Here goes! Hope for the best!' And he swung the nearest handle round from left to right. There was a clash of controlled steam and as he began to pull and turn everything in sight in the opposite direction, he heard the wheels screaming as they locked beneath him. Bill Jelly watched aghast as the engine trundled towards the buffers, losing speed, but not fast enough; he shut his eyes and put his hands over his ears but this didn't stop him hearing a rending crash and a last dismal wail on the whistle.

On Platform One Kathy was trying to pacify an hysterical Mr Jenkins. 'You can't open a railway without a train,' he was bleating, 'and we haven't got our uniforms yet and we're supposed to start playing in eleven and a half minutes!' Kathy took him by the arm and led him to the Parcels Office. She told him to sit down and have a cup of tea and he burst into tears. 'We must all stand together, Mr Jenkins, in this hour of trial. My husband will sort it out, never fear – but we must keep our end up – we can't disappoint all these people.' She looked up the platform to where Jan and Jessica were talking to a group of twenty or thirty people queueing outside the station gate. Kathy said, 'Now you have your tea, Mr Jenkins, and then get your uniform on and start playing at eleven-forty on the dot.' She raised her voice, calling to Jan, 'I should let them in now – there're refreshments ready here if anybody wants some.' She went on thinking to herself, 'And as things are going that's about all they'll get today. . . .'

Bob and Jimmy pumped the maintenance truck along the platform by Stogumber Halt and Basil swung aboard as they passed him. He said breathlessly, 'About five minutes ago – goodness knows what's happened by now!' Then he began helping Bob and Jimmy in turn to swing at the wheel jack.

Bill and a shaken Commander looked at the front of the Flyer. Luckily little damage had been done, but the force of the engine even at its last moments had pushed the struts of the buffers back and the front wheels lay just off the end of the rails – only an inch – but, as Bill said, it might as well have been a mile. Nothing short of an elephant would be able to pull it back on the rails and there weren't many elephants in Somerset at that time of year. He and Jack Frost turned as the maintenance truck came bonking down towards them and braked just back of the points. The Commander looked very pink and very ashamed. 'Blue blistered binnacles, I'd rather anything had happened than this . . . I only wanted to pretend.' Bob Carter looked really angry as he said, 'Yes. You've pretended us clean out of our Grand Opening. It was due to start in thirty-one minutes.' Jimmy nudged him. 'Dad – what's up with Bill?' Bob glanced towards the tramp whose eyes were staring and his mouth opening and shutting. At last he raised a shaking hand and pointed. The others followed his gaze.

Along a track on the edge of the cutting three men were leading six great cart-horses. They were be-ribboned and be-brassed and coats shining like silk and manes and tails combed and plaited and each one looked like an equine king. Bill found his voice, 'They must be on their way to the Taunton Show.' Bob snapped into action. 'Jimmy – run up and stop them – tell them our tale and see if they can help!' Jimmy was off like a rocket as Bob turned, calling, 'The rest of us – get all the ropes and chains we can find and link them on the rear of the Flyer just in case.' As they rushed to shackle up, Bob saw Jimmy finish talking to the leading man, who turned to his companions, and they started to bring their magnificent charges down the path to the junction, bells and harness jingling merrily. Within moments, everyone jumping like grasshoppers to help, the six beasts were harnessed to the rear of the Flyer. The three horsemen urged the creatures with encouraging oaths and cheers and one cracked his whip in the air. As they strained, gravel and stones flew from under the huge pounding hooves. Nothing happened for a while, and then slowly, unbelievably, the six tons of muscled magnificence began to heave the engine back on the track. Bob watched amazed as the front wheels inched back on to engage the lines, then, in a ponderous rush, the engine rolled back along the track behind the horses.

Flockton Station was gay and forlorn at the same time. The flags fluttered, the bunting billowed and the bright shirts and skirts of the crowd shimmered like a flower garden. All the tickets had been sold and Kathy was doing a bumper trade in buns, sandwiches, teas, ices; but Mr Jenkins's band, as the hands of the station clock crept nearer to eleven-forty-five, played more and more slowly and lugubriously till their selection from *Annie get your Gun* began to sound like Chopin's 'Funeral March'.

Kathy, Jan and Jessica stood in a miserable clump together when all at once – over the mournful mooing of the trombone – came the cheerful 'Whhoo-oo-ooo!' of the Flyer. Geoff Gosling sprang forward to release the opening tape as the Flyer thumped backwards through the gaping crowd and slowed, and joined with a satisfying 'doi-oi-ing' the coaches standing waiting on Platform One. A great cheer went up. The band started to accelerate as Mr Jenkins's hands waved faster matching his delighted heart-beats, and Bob jumped down and rapped out instructions. Commander Frost plucked his willowy wife from the crowd and towed her to the dais. Jimmy blew on his whistle. Jan and Jessica called, 'All aboard!' and the people with tickets swarmed in through all the doors. Bill had been persuaded after all not to let his skiffle group down, and he joined Jimmy and Tink Filmer on the flat truck behind the coaches.

Commander Frost looked at his watch. 'Eleven-fifty-eight and a half! No time for speeches, Althea! Bash the bubbly on the bows!' Althea Frost swung the bottle and those people still on the platform who had simply come to watch gave another cheer

as the bottle smashed on the flanks of the Flyer. As Althea cut
the tape, another cheer! The Commander dashed back to the flat
truck where Jimmy was holding out his washboard.

Jimmy caught Mr Jenkins's eye and the diminutive minstrel
raised his baton. Jimmy blew on the whistle again, Jan waved the
green flag and swung on to the footplate beside Bob, Kathy and
Jessica as the band and the group broke into the 'Song of the
Flyer'. Bob let loose the Flyer's power and the engine's happy
heart thumped in time to the beat of the merry music. To cheers
and singing, the engine drew its laughing load slowly up the
platform and on down the line, towards Lane End and a bright
extraordinary future.

The Song of the Flyer

2nd Verse

So here's an invitation
you really can't decline
We leave from Flockton Station
at eleven fifty-nine
All aboard
All aboard
The whistle blows
and there she goes
The Flockton Flyer line
Steam train
Dream train
Smoke 'n flame
Stoke 'n strain
All that's fine
All that's mine
The Flockton Flyer line

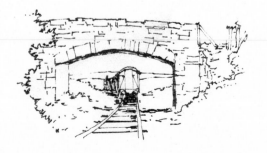